PORTRAIT OF THE WALRUS BY A YOUNG ARTIST

PORTRAIT OF THE

A NOVEL ABOUT ART, BOWLING,

WALRUS

PIZZA, SEX, AND HAIR SPRAY

BY A YOUNG

FROM THE PEN OF LAURIE FOOS

ARTIST

COFFEE HOUSE PRESS :: MINNEAPOLIS

Coffee House Press is supported in part by a grant provided by the Minnesota State Arts Board, through an appropriation by the Minnesota State Legislature, and by a grant from the National Endowment for the Arts, a federal agency. Additional support has been provided by the Lila Wallace-Reader's Digest Fund; The McKnight Foundation; Lannan Foundation; Jerome Foundation; Target Stores, Dayton's, and Mervyn's by the Dayton Hudson Foundation; General Mills Foundation; St. Paul Companies; Honeywell Foundation; Star Tribune/Cowles Media Company; Butler Family Foundation; The James R. Thorpe Foundation; The Beverly J. and John A. Rollwagen Fund of The Minneapolis Foundation; and The Andrew W. Mellon Foundation.

Coffee House Press books are available to the trade through our primary distributor, Consortium Book Sales & Distribution, 1045 Westgate Drive, Saint Paul, MN 55114. For personal orders, catalogs, or other information, write to: Coffee House Press, 27 North Fourth Street, Suite 400, Minneapolis, MN 55401.

LIBRARY OF CONGRESS CIP DATA
Foos, Laurie, 1966-
    Portrait of the walrus by a young artist : a novel / by
Laurie Foos.
        p.   cm.
    ISBN 1-56689-057-8 (alk. paper)
    1. Title.
PS3556.O564P67 199
813'.54--dc21   96-54052
                                                CIP

10   9   8   7   6   5   4   3   2   1

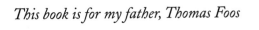

This book is for my father, Thomas Foos

The time has come, the walrus said, to do away with
symbolism, with escapism, purity, innocence, evasion.
                                        —*Federico Fellini*, 8 1/2

Every act of creation is first of all an act of destruction.
                                        —*Pablo Picasso*

CHAPTER ONE

To live a life without walruses in it is to risk a life without redemption. Or, at the very least, to reduce yourself to the quest for the perfect cholesterol level, nothing but salads and line dancing, a bowling ball that fits like a glove. Without the walruses I'm nothing. Or so they would have me think.

There was a time in my life when I thought I could not go on without them. I watched myself on television and played old records in my underwear, tried to drown myself in the bathtub, seal myself up in terra cotta bliss. But Bessie found me every time and brought me back here to my pen and memories.

—from *How to Live Without a Walrus* by Frances Fisk

F I'D KNOWN WALRUSES WERE WAITING FOR ME ON SOME back road in Florida, I might have taken more of an interest in bowling. I might have stopped shutting myself off from the world in order to sculpt sharks in my room, creating only large, mangled beings with lopsided heads and bad teeth. Maybe it would have been best to close my eyes and send my ball spinning down the alley, even if all my efforts wound up in the gutter. But bowling could never be enough for me. There had to be dreams and words, a life unencumbered by pantyhose, bowling shoes, and the constant sting of regret.

Mother wanted me in on her bowling, to dress me up in a pair of pink shoes as I delivered strike after mythical strike. To wipe the clay from my hands and stop talking about my dead father. If I'd only try, she said, I'd see that bowling alleys had more life than I'd ever given them credit for. But I was unwilling to try.

Bessie first sparked the idea in Mother, took her to the alley in downtown Danforth to sign them up for the doubles league. With the insurance my father had left us and the occasional sale of a chainsaw man, we had more than enough money to keep Bessie with us and to live any kind of life we chose. I could have gone to art school, Mother could have traveled around the world. We could have bought Bessie an aquarium of her own and watched the sharks all day long. But all Mother wanted to do was bowl.

By that time my father was a dark memory in the house, Mother having all but eradicated him from the fabric of our lives. She sealed up the basement where he'd lived those last years and sold nearly all of his *Men With Chainsaws* to local museums. All day long she waxed the wood floors with a toothbrush to polish off the clay residue that might have been left behind. She said that having to live under the shadow of an artist was too much to ask of any woman.

"I gave him what may well have been the best years of my life, Frances," she said, "and now I want a little for myself."

When Bessie first suggested bowling as an alternative to her life of cleaning, Mother resisted. There was simply too much cleaning to do, she said. She could smell clay in the air, see the chalky residue when she blew her nose into pure white handkerchiefs. Bessie and I knew that what she'd been smelling was not my father's clay at all, but the sharks

I'd been trying to sculpt in my bedroom, though telling her this might have cracked the thin veneer of her bowler's persona.

"There's not enough clay left in this world," Bessie said, "for all the smelling you say you do."

Bessie winked and flashed me a secret smile. I bit my nails in the corner and tried not to laugh.

I kept my father's wood work table in my bedroom and hoarded pounds of terra cotta wrapped in wax paper in my closet. At night before I went to bed I spread out my tools—a bowl of water for keeping the clay wet, brushes and sponges to add texture, and rolled-up newspaper to fill the bodies of the sharks, to keep the clay from sagging and flaking off their unfinished bodies. My father had always padded his figures with newspaper before depositing them in the kiln—partly to round out the torso while drying and to prevent the figure from bursting, and partly because he said it thrilled him to know that after firing, inside the figure was nothing but a heap of ash.

I let my sharks dry in the closet when I was finished, hanging pairs of jeans and old blazers on wilted hangers to conceal them. I made hammerheads and tigers, great whites that grew hard and crusty from lack of water. At night I sprayed them with water bottles to touch up their flaws, but still the bodies became dented and sagged. I dug deep black eyes into the sides of their heads with my father's steel palettes to give them the illusion of breathing. But none of them ever came out right. The harder I tried to perfect their elongated bodies, to smooth out fins and sloping backs, the more misshapen they became. Their fins were knotty, their backs gnarled, heads too large, and mouths full of chipped teeth. With each failure I wept and carried them out behind the garage where Bessie and I hid them under old picnic tables and rotted two-by-fours that Mother had never called the town to collect. Each time another fin broke off in my hand, I wept for the grief it must have cost my father to part with each one of his sculptures. It was no wonder that he'd ended up the way he did.

THEY ARGUED about bowling for some time, but eventually Mother relented. Together they joined a league, and out they went into the world every Thursday night. They wore matching pink bowling shirts and leg warmers, Bessie's warm brown skin smooth under all that glaring pinkness. She wore a woolen headband around her head to keep her hair from kinking and Mother did hers up in a chignon, a high blonde helmet with lacquered curls that hung down over her brow. Bessie and I both felt the chignon was too formal for bowling but we kept it to ourselves, encouraging her as she sprayed her hair with a fury and scuffed the hardwood floors with her borrowed bowling shoes. Wherever she moved her feet she left shreds of rubber that gripped the floor like paste. Then Mother would have to get down on her hands and knees and polish the floor with lemon oil and a cheesecloth, peering at the finish until her reflection reappeared beneath her hand. Only then did she smile up at Bessie and take off the bowling shoes, tiptoeing across the room in her knee-highs to keep her feet from sliding out from under her.

Occasionally they dragged me along with them, and I would sit in a plastic chair totaling up their strikes and spares, smiling on cue when Mother introduced me to a toothless woman who had the distinction of having once bowled a perfect game. In the margins of their score sheets I kept a tally of the months—thirty-six, the time it would take for four pregnancies—that had passed since my father's death, and the five weeks left until my eighteenth birthday. When I turned eighteen, I told myself, my real life would finally begin. Until then, I thought of life at the bowling alley as a kind of purgatory.

ONE THURSDAY NIGHt Mother took a long time getting ready for bowling. It was the anniversary of my father's death and an article had appeared in the local paper. TOWN MARKS THE ANNIVERSARY OF THE DEATH OF MORTON FISK—HIS *MEN WITH CHAINSAWS* THE EMBODIMENT OF THE UNCONSCIOUS MIND IN CONFLICT WITH ITSELF. Ordinarily Mother would have torn the headline off the page and burned it in the kitchen with a match, leaving a cloud of sulfur hanging in the air as a reminder of all she'd been through. But this time she folded it neatly and left it outside my bedroom door.

When I thanked her, she only said, "He was your father, Frances, whether I like it or not."

And then she put on her bowling shoes and went about the business of twisting up her hair. I could hear her spraying it and combing it out again, along with the phlegmy squirting of mousse. Although she claimed to be assaulted by the slightest hint of clay in the air, apparently the clouds of aerosol spray didn't make her the least bit queasy. I sat outside the door leading down to the basement and read the article, counting the minutes until it was time for them to leave.

"With his brilliant realization of man's inner conflicts—the constant battle waged between the primitiveness of the id and the gentility of the super ego—Morton Fisk will be remembered as one of the twentieth century's major artists. Fisk's Men With Chainsaws, *plastic earth figures coupled with aluminum chainsaws which symbolize the often violent impulses of the id,*

personify the unconscious struggle inherent in mankind. No artist has since equaled the raw earthiness of Fisk's vision, a vision which the artist himself came to embody in his much heralded return to natural life, a life which refused to be imposed upon by societal conventions. Though his life and death have since been marked by sensationalism and myth, the art world will forever mourn the purity of his genius and the valiant battle he waged to unleash the collective unconscious of mankind."

BESSIE WOULD have done anything for Mother, and for me of course, but for different reasons. To a certain degree she looked at Mother as a kind of savior because she'd rescued her from her job at an aquarium where she explained shark habits to school tours. With a plastic fin on her head she mimicked their movements through the water, held up synthetic skins for the kids to touch. Hers was a hands-on exhibit. Mother and I had gone there one day to watch the dolphin show, sat in the front row huddled together while the dolphins splashed in the air and bounced shiny red balls on their snouts. When they landed we were covered in the heavy spray, and before I had a chance to laugh or dry myself off, Mother had me by the hand and was pulling me out toward the shark exhibit. She was crying, though at the time I didn't understand why. Without looking at me she sat down on a bench with her face in her hands, her shoulders shaking with sobs.

For a minute I stood there staring down at her, wanting to sit down and put my arm around her, to tell her it was all going to be all right. But I knew that would have been a lie. Out of the corner of my eye I saw Bessie, a black woman with a shark's fin on her head and a crowd of kids all around her. Before I could stop myself I ran toward her and pushed my way through the crowd.

"Something's wrong with my mother," I said, tears welling in my eyes. She looked down at me and followed me out to the bench where Mother sat in her rumpled overcoat, chewing at her fingernails and rocking herself back and forth. Bessie got down on her haunches and took both of Mother's hands, and I moved back toward the shark tanks while they sat huddled together, their foreheads touching. I never knew what they said to each other that day, but for weeks afterward we went back to the aquarium where I'd listen to Bessie's shark talk and then she and Mother would huddle under the stand where they sold helium balloons whispering to each other. She came to live with us as a kind of companion—an assistant, Mother said—scrubbing her way through the house and trying her best to hold us together while my father went to pieces in the basement.

Later when I asked Bessie if she missed the aquarium, she'd only say, "Except for you, Frances, most kids don't know the first thing about sharks."

Bessie had bought Mother a new bowling ball to take her mind off of things. She'd saved her salary (what Mother liked to call her "stipend," as if she were a graduate student or even an artist in training) for several weeks to buy Mother a ball with her name engraved on it. She'd even had it polished and sized by bringing Mother's rings along with her. All the best bowlers had them. There was nothing like a new bowling ball, Bessie said, to remind you of how good you had it. She sat down next to me on the stairs and unzipped the bowling bag, slowly, like a seduction, all the time giggling in her throat.

"They don't come much brighter than this," she said, reaching in to lift the magenta ball from its bag.

The ball shone under the lights, the colors spinning through the hallway as Bessie turned it around and around in her hands. Violet, yellow, and green reflected high over our heads. Above the holes drilled especially for Mother's fingers appeared her name, *Arlene*, engraved in gray letters.

"Think she'll like it?" Bessie asked, framing the ball with her brown hands.

For a long time I sat staring at it, watching the colors move under the light, shading my eyes from its blinding pinkness. I wanted to say yes, that she'd like it fine, that it would certainly help her forget about my father and maybe even improve her game. My panties choked me around the waist, making it hard to breathe. *What if my whole life turned out to be a gutter ball?* I wanted to say, but instead I just let my mouth hang open, a sob stuck in my throat.

We sat there for awhile without speaking, just staring down at our feet while Bessie hummed a little in her throat. I reached inside the waistband of my pants and fingered the indentations left from the tightness of my panties. I always wore them two sizes too small to remind me of the pain I'd been through. They'd squeeze the life out of me if I wasn't careful. Sometimes there was nothing I wanted more.

"I'm ready for my surprise," Mother called. She bounded into the living room in her bowling shirt and a pair of pink bowling shoes, her hair sprayed so thickly that it wouldn't move. The spray cast a net over her hair, squeezing it into a tight bunch on top with curls that hung uneasily on either side of her face. You could smell the mousse from across the room.

Bessie handed Mother the bowling bag. For a minute Mother just stared at us, but then she unzipped the bag all of a sudden and pulled the ball out, shrieking with laughter and doing a little dance around the room. The bowling shoes left scuff marks everywhere her heels touched the floor, but in her excitement she didn't seem to notice.

"Take my picture, Bessie," she said, giggling, high-pitched and breathless. I hadn't heard her laugh that way in years.

Bessie ran for the Polaroid and took shots of Mother in various poses, with her knees bent and her feet pointed as if she were ready to bowl a strike; holding the ball up near her face and blinking her eyes like a fashion model.

"You can't get much further away from art than this," she said, the flash lighting up the room as she preened and giggled with the ball.

I looked down at my watch and told them they were going to be late for their league if they didn't hurry, but Mother just waved her hand like they had all the time in the world.

"Take one more of Frances and me," she said.

I glanced over at Bessie and shook my head. What would my father say, I wondered, if he'd known that we'd come to this? Standing in the living room with a bowling ball posing for family pictures. I was the one he counted on to understand him, I wanted to say, but Bessie said to get into the picture with Mother and not put up a fuss. So I said nothing, just shuffled over to Mother and tried my best to smile.

"Say 'cheese,'" Bessie said, and we both laughed at the pun. The flash was blinding.

"Don't wait up," Mother called, as she hurried out of the house ahead of Bessie, dragging her new bowling ball and bag behind her.

I walked toward my room, leaving the scattered Polaroids over the living room floor. The smell of hair spray left a sickness in my throat.

"Frances," Bessie called as I opened the door to my room, "bowling isn't the worst thing a mother can do."

I closed the door behind me and sat cross-legged on the floor with a thick wad of clay in my lap. The thud of the dead bolt reverberated through the house. I knew that Bessie was right, that Mother was entitled to live whatever kind of life she saw fit. I didn't resent her for that, and in fact was happy that she'd found something besides clean-ing to give her life purpose. I stood up and took off my blouse and jeans and sat there in my bra and tight panties, kneading the clay in my palms, rolling it around and around into a ball. It occurred to me then that this was how it was to be for us now that bowling had wound its way into our lives.

LATER THAT NIGHT I went into Mother's room and rum-maged through her drawers. My heart pounded as I lifted her cotton panties and silky bras, searching under her socks and pantyhose for clues—to what, I wasn't sure, but the urge to keep looking got hold of me and it took all I had not to turn her drawers over on the carpet and run my hands through the piles of shiny underpants.

Mother's alarm clock ticked on her dresser as if to remind me of the time that had gone by since my father had died. I opened each drawer slowly and quietly, imagin-ing that Mother was sleeping and might catch me at any time, although I knew she and Bessie weren't even into the second game of the night. I imagined Mother spinning her ball down the alley and laughing in her pink shoes while I had my hands in her panties, trying to hold on to whatev-er was left of my father.

When I got to the last drawer I had to crouch down on my haunches and pull with both arms. The wood was cracked around the sides and moaned as I tried to force it open. I dug both feet into the carpet and arched my back, leaning back with all my weight. Beads of sweat formed on my forehead and upper arms. The drawer suddenly gave way, the wood splintered onto the carpet. I landed flat on my back.

For a minute I lay stunned, my feet in the air and my hair spread over the carpet. When I sat up, my hair crackled with static. I crawled over to the drawer slowly, trying to catch my breath. There were tiny pieces of wood all over Mother's beige carpet, pale and chipped like sawdust. And then I smelled it, the wind moving up my nostrils and bringing a familiar tightness to my chest.

"My God," I said out loud.

Men With Chainsaws. There were nearly twenty of them strewn inside the drawer. Some were wrapped in old newspaper, the paper crackling in my hands as I gingerly lifted one of the figures out of the box. Bits of the newspaper crumbled away and floated down to the carpet. Some of the headlines dated back more than ten years. A few figures were chipped in the faces and the long slender toes that my father was famous for. Many of them were covered in shards of his briefs, the elastic tied tightly around their heads like bandages. Inside the elastic bands, the word HANES stood out, the blue letters having yet to fade despite time and utter neglect. The men were varied in size, from about ten inches high to some that couldn't have been taller than an inch or two. I picked up one of the smaller ones and pressed it to my nose, breathing in the clay. When I moved it away from my face, the metal tooth of a chainsaw pricked the end of my nose. I lifted a scrap of underwear from the drawer and dabbed at the thin line of blood.

I stood up and looked in the mirror over Mother's dresser. The scratch on my nose was thin and fine, the tiny blade of the chainsaw having left its mark along the length of my nose. For a long time I stood staring at myself, at my pale complexion and shining dark eyes, the reddish tint of my hair.

I put the men back the way I found them, wrapping them in elastic and arranging them as haphazardly as Mother had seemed to. I was just about to put the last one back when I saw the inscription on the base of one of the sculptures. In a fine scrawling print were the words, *For Frances.* It was no wonder Mother had been hiding them, I thought. He'd saved this one for me.

I set the figure down on Mother's dresser and went out to the hall closet for the vacuum. Blood thumped in my jaw as I thought about all the time and energy she'd put into keeping his work from me. How long had they been stifled inside that drawer, piled one on top of the other with no treated cloth to protect them, not even a layer of cellophane? I dragged the vacuum into her room, letting the hose bounce against the walls, pressing hard so that the wheels would leave their telltale trace behind. With both arms I pushed the vacuum over and over the splinters until the belt crackled, sparks flying out from the wheels. When all the wood was gone I lifted the chainsaw man and tucked him inside my T-shirt, the cool metal pressed against my skin. I slammed the hall closet door as hard as I could, even though I knew there was no one home to hear me.

I rushed back to my room and took out the clay hidden in the back of my closet. With the chainsaw man sitting on my bed, I worked all night, closing my eyes and praying that the sharks would come, their enormous teeth sinking into the recesses of my brain. My hands moved of their own accord, and I didn't stop, even after I heard Mother's key in the door and the soft sounds of Bessie's laughter.

I know what you've done, I wanted to say, but instead I kept my eyes closed, my hands moving, fingers thrust in the heavy wad of clay.

When I heard Mother close the door to her bedroom some time later, I finally opened my eyes. This was the moment I'd been waiting for, I thought: an inspiration from beyond the grave. I felt my shoulders slump and a chill run down my spine as I looked at what I'd created. In the middle of the floor sat an enormous reddish bowling ball just as round and perfect as it could be. I moved my hands over my face, smearing the clay over my cheeks and under my eyes. I wiped my face on the back of my sleeve and felt the scratch on my nose come open, a thin line of blood moving down over my lip and leaving tiny red drops on the bowling ball.

I washed my hands in a bowl of water, letting the clay move in swirling motions off my hands and fingernails. Then, before I got into bed, I slipped the metal chainsaw out from the grip of the figure's hands. Slowly I carved Mother's name under the enormous finger holes, sliding the chainsaw over the wet clay, dipping it in and then wiping the excess on my panties. When I was finished I peeled off my T-shirt and rolled the bowling ball next to the open window to let it dry in the night air. I slept with the lights on that night and the first thing I saw in the morning was the enormity of the perfect ball and Mother's name in block letters, bigger than life.

CHAPTER TWO

As daughters we dream of our fathers with bowling balls
for heads, pizza sauce dripping from their open, wanting
mouths.

Some of them are artists, some not, all of them in their
underpants. They live their whole lives underwater, the
only sign of them their long wrinkled snouts quivering in
the air.

AT THE PEAK OF HIS CAREER MY FATHER TOOK
TO wearing nothing but briefs and sculpting
where no one could see him. I'd always found it
odd that someone's life could have been at such polar
opposites, so full of wonder and yet cut off from the world.
During that time my father's men had appeared in every
major museum in the country, his face on every art magazine on the newsstands, and yet each day his screams
became more filled with artistic abandonment and terror.

"They'll cut off my penis with a chainsaw!" he'd scream.
"Only my underwear can save me!"

At night when it was quiet I sometimes woke to find him
standing at the foot of my bed, clay flaking off his heaving
chest. At first I thought it was a dream, but then I'd catch a
glimpse of the fly of his briefs twitching, his eyes wide. I'd

hold my breath and stare at him as he moved in front of my window, the moonlight coming through the venetian blinds. In the half-light of the room the swell of his belly was enormous, the thick folds of flesh hanging over the waistband of his briefs. All he did in these last years was eat, until his waist had expanded and hung down like a huge pouch of flesh-colored gel. His stomach shook as he stood there in the window, humming low in his throat and padding over to the edge of my bed. Wiry hairs, a hint of rubbery flesh poked through the slot of his briefs. My heart pounded under the covers, my throat dry. He'd turn to me then, his feet slapping against the hardwood floors as he smiled down at me, his front teeth edging over his parched bottom lip.

"What is it, Dad?" I'd whisper, propping myself up on my elbows. "What do you want?"

And he'd stare down at me, his eyes so dark I could barely make out the pupils. Deep lines dripped down his cheeks and pulled his mouth down.

"Some water," he'd say. "All I want is some water."

I moved past him to the bathroom and filled a flowered Dixie cup to the brim. Carefully I tiptoed back to the room, cupping my left hand underneath to catch the drops. By the time I got back to the bedroom he was gone, the only remaining trace a lingering smell of clay in the air. I'd stand in the kitchen staring at the locked basement door and then I'd hear the scream, deep and open-mouthed. There was nothing like it. I imagined him kneeling on the cold slab floor with his head back and his teeth bared, his throat opening up. If only he'd let me down there, I thought, I could save him. But the door never opened. Before Mother could find me I'd leave the cup outside the basement door and hurry back to bed, pulling the covers over my head and waiting for the screams to end.

ON THE last night of the season, Mother insisted that I come to watch her and Bessie bowl. She called me into her bedroom and fixed her hair while I sat on the bed and watched. She had on a tight white blouse with a white lacy bra underneath that I recognized from her dresser, the kind with thin underwire cups and a come-hither puff of lace along the edges. You could see this lace as she stood in front of the mirror to smooth her chignon, talking all the time about the pleasure she got from bowling, the sheer mindlessness of it all.

"Before bowling, my life was nothing but art," she said to me in this plaintive voice. "This is the beginning of a whole new world for us, you just wait and see."

I sat on the edge of the bed and watched as she slid on pink pantyhose and matching pink bowling shoes, the lace bra glowing all the time under her sheer white shirt. It had been several weeks since the night I'd sculpted the bowling ball, and since then I'd wandered through the house in a kind of daze, waiting for something to happen. She'd stopped complaining about the smell of clay.

I looked down at the broken drawer where I'd found my father's sculptures. She hadn't mentioned my thievery or acted like she missed the shreds of his briefs, and if she had, I'd been too sunk in the depths of my despair to have heard her. Besides, I thought, the figure was meant for me. I had no intention of letting her discard it with the rest of my father's memory.

Just then she turned to me and gave me a half-smile, her lips turned up at the edges, as if she didn't trust herself to show me a full, bright set of teeth. She bent down and passed her fingers through my bangs, a tiny wisping movement, the way my father had touched me when I was a little girl. He used to mess my bangs with his clay-lined fingertips, and then I'd stare at myself in the mirror, smiling at the terra cotta peels he'd left in my hair.

It was as if for that one moment, she knew.

"Go on and wait with Bessie," she said. "Watching us bowl will do you a world of good."

I wandered out into the kitchen and found Bessie icing a cake in the shape of a bowling ball. She looked startled when she saw me, and dropped her knife into the vat of pearly icing.

"What's the occasion?" I said, nudging Bessie with my elbow, but she shooed me away and handed me a spoonful of icing to taste.

"It's nothing," Bessie said, not looking at me. She stuck pink toothpicks into the cake and wrapped it in cellophane before shoving it inside the refrigerator. I lapped at the sweetness of the icing, my tongue curling around the spoon in long swirls.

Mother called to us from the front door and I dropped the spoon in the sink, frosting thick on my tongue. We hurried out to the front door. I lingered a minute there, taking my time to turn off the lights and look around at the living room, the shine of the wood floors from all the years of Mother's fervent waxing. The pungent smell of lemon oil and wax permeated the air. The shine was so bright that I could see my reflection even in the dark. If you didn't know better, I thought, you'd think we lived in a bowling alley.

THE BEST THING about bowling was the pizza. I sat at the snack bar and ate it while Mother and Bessie settled into their lane and waved to their friends in the league, men with pot bellies that hung down over their tool belts, thick red tattoos lining their arms—the kind of men some reviewers said my father had satirized in his sculptures, but who were, as my father believed, the essence of life. A man who could operate a chainsaw was as close to real living as you could get, he said. Men like that knew how to keep things manageable, to cut things down to size. They could take a tree and reduce it to strips you could carry in your hands. There was no pretense with that kind of man. Nothing in life could ever remain too much to handle.

I had to sneak to the snack bar when Mother wasn't looking because she said it was in bad taste for her daughter to be seen sitting alone that way with a Coke and a slice of pizza. "Like you're on the make," she said, "and you and I both know you're not." But I just laughed when she said that and ate even more slices for spite. Sometimes the beer-bellied men would stare at me and I'd purposely wolf down a slice, giving them a smile filled with cheese.

Secretly I knew Mother wanted me to stay away from fats because of my father. After he became famous he grew more and more huge, his body seeming to expand with every passing day. Bessie was forever telling her to leave me alone, that junk food was part of a seventeen-year-old's way of life.

"That and sex," Bessie said, "and you should be glad she's not doing that."

The closest I'd ever come was with a boy in junior high school named Frank who used to tease me about my father's art in a throaty voice and kiss me outside my bedroom window. Once he came for me in the night and we held each other on the grass. He got on top of me and pressed my hands into the narrow bones of my shoulders. When we kissed he whimpered a little, muffling his sounds in the hollow of my neck. Once I licked his ear and he groaned, moving harder against me. He tasted like the sea. He slid his hands over my belly and lifted my T-shirt, dipping his cool fingers inside the waistband of my jeans. I cried out then, and we heard my father scream from inside the house, the basement window steamy from the heat of the kiln.

"It's my father," I said, and he tried to hold on to me, brushing his knuckles over my satin bra, but I was cold. When I tasted salt on his breath, I tried hard not to gag.

"I've got to go in now," I whispered, and ran through the dark with my T-shirt hanging loose at my waist, panties rumpled in the seat of my jeans. I just wanted to get back inside the house and close the windows, shove my hands into a wad of damp clay and wait for him to disappear.

Needless to say, he never came back.

THEY WERE halfway into the fifth frame when I noticed something was wrong. As designated scorekeeper, I sat at the slanted table in a plastic chair and doodled open-mouthed sharks in the margins next to the strikes and spares. The pizza had made me nauseous, and I felt the familiar yearning to be alone in my bedroom where I could strip down and sculpt. I still fought to keep up the pretense, although as far as I could tell the sharks had all but deserted me. I'd been reduced to making bowling balls instead. The sharks no longer came to me, even when I was alone in my bedroom with the bathroom water running next door to create the illusion of being in a tank. When I closed my eyes, my throat felt tight, closed up. I wondered if I were going to drown.

"Isn't this fun, Frances?" Mother called to me each time she placed her feet on the arrows and aimed for the pins.

I nodded at her and sipped at my Coke, and Bessie rolled her eyes when she thought I wasn't looking. Anyone who had known us would know that fun had never entered our lives, and that we'd never given it much thought. It was difficult to have fun when you were constantly waiting for your father to emerge, sweaty and full of dreams, from the basement where he'd sealed himself in. Art had left little room for fun, as far as we were concerned.

Between each frame Mother disappeared behind the bar and wouldn't come back until it was her turn again. When I asked Bessie where she was, she made some off-hand compliment about the sharks I was doodling.

"Your mother's having some fun, sugar," she said, leaning on the word fun, like it was some sort of private joke between us, though I didn't get it.

And then I saw the kind of fun Bessie meant. It was Mother's turn, and I took a long swallow of Coke while I waited for her to take her place at the lane. Bessie put her arm around me and squeezed my shoulder, hard. Soda beads dribbled down the front of my cotton shirt.

"What is it?" I asked, looking up from the scoreboard.

Mother stood in front of me with her sheer blouse shining under the lights, her chignon casting an oblong shadow on the overhead scoreboard. She smiled at me, wide, her teeth and gums glowing.

"Frances, I'd like you to meet Stan," she said.

She stepped aside like a showgirl and held her arms out to present him to me. At first it didn't register, and I kept staring up at the shadow of her hair over the scoreboard and that lacy bra poking from beneath her blouse. Her teeth had never looked more enormous.

"Pleased to meet you," the voice said.

Bessie poked at my arm, and I dropped my pencil on the floor. It rolled away with a soft pinging sound. I looked up at the hand thrust in my face and shook it with the little strength I could muster.

"Likewise," I said. The sound of my own voice was a shock. Mother grinned maniacally, and I took a long swig of Coke,

letting the harsh bubbles bring tears to my eyes. The voice
kept on, chatting about the importance of bowling and what
a wonderful woman my mother was. I felt myself nodding,
and was vaguely aware of Bessie patting my leg beneath the
table, rhythmic pats that were somewhere between comfort
and irritation. I wanted to turn my head to have a look at
him, to see whether his eyes were dark or light, whether they
moved in synch with Mother's movements. I stole a glance
below his belt buckle to see if underwear lines were visible
through his cotton pants, but the pants were too loose, the
material pouching out from the waist and around the hips as
if he knew what I was after. All I could do was hold on to the
paper cup and let Bessie pat me while I stared up at the shadow of Mother's hair dwarfing the scoreboard.

I smiled at him and he smiled back, his teeth jagged at
the edges.

"She's one hell of a bowler," he said.

I raised my cup as a measure of politeness. When I lowered my arm again, my wrist shook, and the soda poured
out in a thick brown splash over my feet. He laughed then,
a kind of conspiratory laugh, but Mother just glared at me,
as if I were a little girl who had just wet herself in front of
a house full of company.

IN THE CAR on the way home I sat in the back seat alone.
The Coke had left a sticky film over my shoes. I pressed my
feet together at the toes and pulled them apart over and
over again to hear the smack of the rubber soles come
together and let go. My father's body had made this same
sound when they lifted him off the floor: a sharp sucking of
skin. I tried to concentrate on this sound while Mother
chattered on about Stan, the bowling kingpin. He owned
three bowling alleys and had one on the way, she said with

a chuckle in her voice. His real name was Stanley Robert Boardman, and he was a bowler's dream.

Apparently he'd come to Connecticut scouting possible sites for a spread of bowling alleys in the Northeast. He was from Florida, but felt that the change of seasons and the cool night air up here might be a haven for closet bowlers, the ones who had been waiting all their lives to bowl but had been diverted along the way by bad habits or faulty dreams. It turned out he missed the easy access to the ocean too much to consider the prospect seriously, much as his heart ached at the lack of high-tech alleys in the greater Danforth area. He'd seen Mother on the one night he visited our local alley and said he liked her form. And from what I could see, Mother liked his as well.

"Oh, Bessie," she whispered, as if for some reason she thought I couldn't hear her in the back seat, "it was like he came here just to find me. 'Me, Stan,' I told him, 'I'm one of the people you came to save.'"

Mother was a great believer in fate, which was why she fought so hard to keep me from following what she thought was destined to be mine. Nothing was written in stone, she liked to say. There was always room to fight. Yet I could see that already she was surrendering herself to what she believed was meant for her, a life that I could hardly imagine, a life spent trying to keep bowlers in their own lanes.

I sat looking at the headlights in the distance and took a deep breath. I thought of Stan's hand, wondered what that hand would feel like if it were ever to brush its fingers through my bangs. Slowly I tilted my palm up under my nose to see what sort of scent it had left on me. You could tell a lot about a man by the smell of his hands, Bessie liked to say. I took a deep breath through my nostrils and let the air move out my open mouth. It smelled dark and rubbery, as dead as a bowling ball.

The next time I saw the Kingpin, as Bessie and I had begun to call him behind Mother's back, he was dressed in a three-piece pinstripe suit, his hair slicked back. Mother was having a party for some of her bowling friends, and the Kingpin was the guest of honor.

"Welcome to our home," Mother said in a breathy whisper as she opened the door and guided the Kingpin into our lives. She pressed against him as she took his coat. He had on a black cowboy hat with the sides turned up and a pair of wingtips that scraped against the wooden floor. He gave Mother a secret smile, his jagged teeth flashing. He pressed his lips to Bessie's cheek, leaving a wet smack on the side of her face. For me he offered his hand and squeezed hard when I took it. I sauntered off in the corner to sniff it, but Mother caught me and pulled my hand away.

"He's never been within five miles of a piece of clay in his life," she whispered. "Don't even think about it."

For the party Mother had spent the last twelve hours on her hands and knees polishing the floors with a cheese cloth wrapped around a fistful of paste wax. Bessie had stood over her with her hands on her hips, shaking her head and clucking her tongue.

"These floors will be so slippery, half the party will fall right on their butts," Bessie said, but Mother wouldn't listen, and just kept right on waxing and whistling a country song she'd been playing on the stereo for the last few days. In addition to being the bowling king, the Kingpin was also a champion line dancer.

"If she starts wearing a cowboy hat," Bessie said, "Lord help us."

When the other guests arrived—a woman with tall black hair and a space in her teeth, a man in his early fifties with a mermaid tattooed on his arm, a couple of the men with beer bellies and tool belts, and a redhead who wore a bandanna tied around her head and called Bessie "darlin"— Bessie and I retreated to the kitchen where she put the finishing touches on the bowling ball cake. I sat on a stool and listened to the chatter in the next room, despite myself. They were talking about the ten pin, how you should never hit the ten pin head on, and about how to make the seven-ten split, which Mother said she'd always thought was impossible.

"Nothing is impossible," the Kingpin said cryptically.

Mother laughed at this, high-pitched and nervous, a bit forced, but a laugh nevertheless. There had never been much laughter in our house when my father was alive. According to Mother, my father laughed at only two kinds of events—during sex, and after he'd finished another of his chainsaw men.

"He laughed only in moments of triumph," she said. "The rest of his life he spent screaming."

I could remember the screams as clearly as if I'd heard them yesterday, but somehow the laughter had escaped me.

Bessie handed me a can of pink frosting to spread on the bowling cake. She always seemed to know when I was absorbed in thoughts of my father, which was nearly all the time, and never failed to try to draw me out of it.

"What's happening with the sharks?" she whispered, as I laid a heaping blob of frosting on the midsection of the ball and swirled it around. "You haven't given up on them?"

I spread the frosting around with flicking movements of my wrist. Bessie bustled around the kitchen filling up trays of M&Ms and nachos covered in piles of sparkling red salsa. I thought of the bowling ball I'd made the night I'd found the chainsaw men, how the sharks' teeth had left nicks in its near-perfect smoothness. Even without a glaze the bowling ball shone as if there were a light emanating from its center. *And my father believed he could rely on me to understand,* I thought with a laugh, as I applied another layer of pink goo to the cake.

I laid the knife down and turned to Bessie. With my right hand I scooped up a fingerful of the frosting and spread it over my lips like a clown. Bessie looked like she was going to laugh at first, but then she must have seen the look in my eyes and came over to hold my hand.

"How did my father become an artist?" I asked.

Bessie wiped the frosting from my lips with a washcloth, the way she had when she first came to live with us and I'd steal into the kitchen to hear stories about the aquarium. Sometimes she'd take out the old plastic fin and put it on her head, dancing around the kitchen to make me laugh. Then she'd whisper about what it was like to have sharks stare at her through a tank, the kind of life she'd had surrounded by water.

"Art was inside him," she said, laying a hand in mine. "It was the only thing that mattered."

After a minute she let go of my hand and carried a tray of M&Ms into the living room, leaving me there with icing stuck between my fingers, crystals of sugar clinging to my hands.

AT MIDNIGHT Mother peeked into the kitchen and told Bessie and me it was time for the cake. To avoid joining the party, I'd been eating bits of it all night until I'd burrowed a hole the size of my fist, a tunnel running through the middle of the cake. When Bessie saw it she shook her head and tried to seal it shut with globs of frosting. Finally she took a fistful of the icing and shoved it into the opening.

"On a night like this," Bessie said, "your mother won't notice a thing."

Bessie set the cake on the dining room table while the guests oohed and ahhed. The woman with the bandanna clicked her heels together in an odd measure of salute. One of the beer-bellied men belched and let out a low wolf whistle as I walked by. When I glared at him, he grinned at me, his lips spread to reveal the gaps in his teeth.

"Want some pizza?" he mouthed, but I just turned away and sat next to Bessie in the corner. I could smell his salty breath from across the room.

The Kingpin stood in front of the bowling cake and flashed an enormous smile. I looked down at his shoes and saw his teeth reflected in his wingtips. He put his arm around Mother and took a deep breath. We sat on the sofas and waited. I could feel the icing still stuck to my hands.

"Before I met Arlene," the Kingpin began, "bowling alleys were my life. Long lanes and spinning balls. Life was a kind of sport. It was a good life, but a lonely one."

Several of the guests murmured their agreement. The man with the mermaid on his arm wiped a tear from the corner of his eye.

"But Arlene has made me see that bowling doesn't have to be a lonely sporting life. That's why I'm proud to say she's about to share the alley of my life with me by becoming my bride."

I felt Bessie's hand on my arm, squeezing. The bowling alley people stood up, whooping and hollering their congratulations. The man with the beer belly gave me a thumbs-up and blew me a kiss. I leaned against Bessie's arm to steady myself, but she and Mother were locked in an embrace. The Kingpin grabbed Mother around the waist and dipped her like a dancer, his lips coming down over his teeth and pressing themselves to Mother's. When he released her I looked for traces of blood around her lips, a piece of flesh sucked out of her face. Mother reached around to lay a possessive hand on the Kingpin's hips. No matter how hard I strained to see I couldn't make out the slightest hint of an elastic waistband around his hips or an underwear crease along the buttocks.

I felt an odd smile form on my lips and stay there, frozen. I couldn't make it stop. It was as if the whole room had receded and I was no longer a part of it. My body kept sitting there and smiling this stupid smile, but my head was somewhere else. I could hear almost nothing, as if my ears had been stopped-up with clay.

The Kingpin came up to me with this wild grin on his face. He leaned over, his back forming a high arc as he reached down to take my hand. I took a long look at his jagged teeth, the pointed edges and square jaw. His hand closed over mine, cold and ridged with callouses, and then his rubbery lips descended on my cheek. Mother squeezed his bicep with both hands. Her cheeks were smeared with lipstick from all the congratulatory kisses.

"Frances," she said, "don't you have anything to say?"

The smile stayed on my face, my lips pulled tight. Everything seemed blurred, like looking through water.

"Congratulations," I said. Mother pursed her lips and kissed me, her stiff chignon stabbing my ear.

When no one was looking I went over to the cake and shoved my fist into the hole I'd made. I grabbed a handful of frosting and smeared it on one of the paper plates. With my index finger I drew pins and a ball, long arrows pointing. I closed my eyes and tried to draw the outline of a shark, but I could not imagine what it looked like anymore, the image of teeth and fins falling away like a bad dream. No matter how hard I tried, all that would come into my mind was bowling balls, their large and artless forms sinking heavily into my brain.

"What's that you're trying to make?" the man with the beer belly said. He was behind me, breathing on my neck. If I leaned back an inch, I'd have felt his tool belt piercing me in the back.

"Nothing you'd understand," I muttered.

I tore the paper plate into pieces and threw them up in the air. He held his hands out to catch them, but they fell through his fingers and landed in a pile on the floor.

WE SPENT the next several weeks packing for Florida. Mother moved through the house like a woman possessed. Her chignon would not stay in place no matter how many times she sprayed it, so furied were her intentions. At first I considered asking to be left behind, but Bessie said a new start would do all of us some good.

With just one week left until my eighteenth birthday, I wondered what might lie ahead for us in Florida. When Mother broke the news to us, I went to my bedroom and climbed inside my closet, the way I did when I was a little girl, before Bessie had come along to save us. Now that Mother was going to have a new husband (who, as far as we could tell, had never held a wad of clay in his lifetime, let alone considered sealing himself up in a basement), what would be left for Bessie to do? Although Mother had originally convinced her to move in with us in order to help raise me, I was now almost an adult, too old to justify anyone's caretaking. And I was certain that Bessie must have had other dreams, plans that didn't involve bowling or art or scrubbing bathtubs.

My hope was that Bessie and I would be left here at my father's house where I could finally learn to sculpt and

Bessie could act as a kind of liaison between Mother and me, the way she always had. When I told Bessie about my plans, she said that we could all use a change of scenery and that Mother needed help making the adjustments to her new life with the Kingpin.

"It wouldn't be right to abandon her now," she said softly while we swept the basement steps. "Besides, you'll be right on the ocean. Think about all the sharks you might see."

Since the house was in mine and Mother's names, Mother agreed we should put off selling it until I was twenty-one. Until then, I could lie on the beach in Florida or spend my days in the bowling alley, find out what I wanted from life. I knew what I wanted from life already, I told her, but she said that art was out of the question.

"You saw what it did to your father," she said, stabbing her fingers through her chignon. "I will not have that happen to you."

Of course I wouldn't have gone without Bessie. The Kingpin was more than happy to have her along, and Mother said we wouldn't know what we'd do without her. The Kingpin had even set up a bedroom for Bessie next to mine in the Florida house, and offered to double her salary to make Mother happy.

"You can't say no," I told her when Mother and the Kingpin couldn't hear, and then we hugged and hugged.

MY BIRTHDAY, like most things in my life, was not what I'd expected. There was so much packing yet to do and so little time left before the wedding, Mother said, that we'd celebrate it quietly at home, have cake while moving boxes.

"We'll make it up to you when we get to Florida," Mother said, "as soon as everything is settled. You'll see."

I nodded and opened the box she gave me wrapped in

silver foil with the words "Your Special" stenciled across it in
bright red letters, the letter "e" and the apostrophe missing.
Mother had never been much of a speller. She clapped her
hands as I peeled the tape away from the edges, slowly, careful not to tear the wrap. Finally I slid the black velvet box
from between the paper and ran my thumb over the edge.

"Go on, open it," Mother squealed.

Bessie stood at the kitchen sink with her back to us as
she filled a crystal vase with water. She bought me roses
every year in different colors to match each birthday. I
glanced over at her as she trimmed each of the eighteen
roses at the bottom and then placed an aspirin in the water.
They were red this year, she said, because this was the year
I'd discover my true love.

The hinges of the box creaked a little as I opened it.
Inside were a pair of pink rhinestone earrings and a necklace to match. I held them up to the light and sat looking
at them for a minute, wondering why Mother had bought
me these when I'd asked for a bracelet made of baked beads
that they sold in the Danforth Museum gift shop.

"To match your dress for the wedding," she said, and
before I could thank her, she pulled the necklace out of my
hands and fastened it around my neck.

"Look at how pretty she is, Bessie," she said. She ran for
her Polaroid and made me pose in front of the roses with
the earrings on, though they clashed horribly with my
flannel nightgown. For one shot I held a single rose to my
lips while Mother preened in her bowling T-shirt and
jeans, her chignon tight at the back of her head.

"Isn't it great to be eighteen?" Bessie said when Mother
left the room, and then we both laughed a little, though I
could tell that Bessie didn't find it very funny at all.

WHILE WE piled boxes into the living room that night so Bessie could clean out our rooms, the Kingpin arrived to present me with my birthday gift. I pretended not to hear him come in the front door and stood packing up old photographs when I heard his wingtips scraping the floor. I watched him as he stood for awhile outside my bedroom in the hallway, hesitating, moving his hips in the dark. After a time he leaned against the wall with his hips stuck out, rolling a bowling pin between his hands. Slowly he rocked back and forth on his heels, his hips twisting in slow circles as if he were dancing. I set the box down on the floor and walked out to the hall, my heart pounding. The Kingpin was someone who needed to be confronted head-on. He stepped forward and held the pin out to me, a smile playing at the corners of his mouth.

"Frances," he whispered, moving close enough for me to smell Mother's hairspray all over him, "this is for you."

I leaned back against the wall and held my breath. The light from the living room reflected on the wall, the pin casting a giant shadow beside me.

"Thank you," I said, loud enough so Bessie and Mother could hear me, "this is certainly something that I don't have."

He held the pin out to me and dropped it into my hands. I fell forward a bit with the weight of it, and the Kingpin smiled, his teeth glowing. It was smooth and hard, heavy. I moved my hands up the length of it to get a better grip, winced at the sting of a splinter. Mother came around the corner then, her high heels clicking on the floor.

"That's his prize pin," Mother said, running up to the Kingpin and laughing. She switched the light on overhead, and I saw the inscription, *With Best Wishes from Dick Weber,* swirled all over it in black ink. "It's his pride and joy."

I smiled a little and laid it down on one of the boxes. With my teeth I yanked the splinter from the soft flesh of my palm. My panties squeezed around my waist, the seam of my jeans digging in between my legs.

"What do you say, Frances?" Mother said, glaring at me. "Don't you know who Dick Weber is? The greatest bowler who ever lived."

I opened my mouth to say something, but the Kingpin reached out and held Mother by the arm.

"It's all right," he said. "Not everyone can appreciate Dick's greatness." He gave Mother a squeeze and tipped his cowboy hat at me before turning to walk away.

Mother followed me into the bedroom and helped me lift one of the heavier boxes. Together we bent at the knees and grunted, a piece of her thick blonde hair hanging down over one eye. We both laughed and shifted our weight, our feet shuffling as we dragged the box into the living room.

"Eighteen," she said, laughing, pieces of the chignon poking out from the sides of her head. "That's when I thought I had all the answers."

We set the box down and took deep breaths. Mother smiled and brushed her fingers through my bangs.

"Yes," I said, and she put her arm around me and held me there for a minute, her breath against my cheek. I closed my eyes and thought of the shadow on the wall, the gash in my hand where the splinter had been. I moved forward to hug her, but just as I did she turned away and headed for the Kingpin. They stood there with their arms around each other, boxes strewn all over the floor around them.

"Happy Birthday," they said in unison, and I waved a hand as if to say thank you and headed back to my room. With both hands I lifted the bowling pin and lay it on the floor, pushed it with my foot to send it spinning across the room.

I opened my closet and took out the chainsaw man from the box where I'd hidden it. When no one was looking I stood the figure at the edge of my bed and kneeled on the floor. The pin banged against the wall, swung toward me and smacked against my knee. I pressed my lips to the figure's face and took a deep breath, trying to drown out the sounds of Mother and the Kingpin giggling in the hall.

"Happy Birthday," I said over and over again, my lips brushing over the hard unglazed clay, my breath moving over the figure and then coming back inside my open mouth.

I DREAMED THAT NIGHT that my body was made of clay. My father was shaping me with his hands, his fingers moving under my neck and poking holes for my eyes. He pulled a pair of briefs over my head as a hat and laughed. At first I was glad to see him, but then he wanted me to hold the chainsaw for him. I couldn't carry it: it was much too heavy.

"It weighs too much," I said, but he wouldn't listen. He pressed the chainsaw into my hands and forced me to hold it. I tried to lift it, but it pulled my clay arms down, the chainsaw dragging down the length of my legs. He danced around me in his underpants and drank glass after glass of water.

"It's my birthday, Dick," he said. "Can I have a glass of water?"

"My name isn't Dick," I said.

He laughed then and dropped the glass at my feet.

Water and glass splashed up at me, the shards shooting holes through my chest and arms. At first you could hardly see them, but then the holes got bigger and bigger. I screamed until my body disappeared and all that was left was my enormous clay head. The sockets of my eyes opened into finger holes. I tried to close my eyes, but the fingers kept coming, closer, ever closer, until all I could do was scream.

ON THE DAY of the wedding I removed the boxes of clay and dragged them out the door to the dumpster. The Kingpin was standing in the driveway beside a long black limousine, the kind we'd had for my father's funeral, polishing his wingtips and sweating. I'd never seen him so nervous. He waved to me from the end of the driveway but didn't bother to come any closer or to help me with my heavy box. His hair and forehead were lined with sweat; even his teeth gleamed.

What point was there anymore in trying to continue my quest for art? Since the Kingpin had come into our lives, all my dreams of sharks had been wiped clean, like Mother's floors. I felt a heaviness in me as I hoisted the box in the air and listened to the sound of it crashing inside the dumpster. It wasn't sorrow exactly, but a terrible emptiness like the end of a life.

Bessie found me sitting outside on the porch stairs before it was time to go. Mother had insisted we all wear pink dresses and matching shoes. She had the good sense not to wear white; for this I had to give her some credit. Bessie's dress was satin and twitched between her thighs when she walked. Mine was lacy and dug into the elastic of my panties, tickling my backside and making me itch. I had to fight the urge to dig at myself. Bessie sat beside me and handed me a packet of bird seed to throw at Mother and the Kingpin after the ceremony.

"What will I do now, Bessie?" I whispered.

She held the front door open for me and smiled. I took a deep breath, sucking the air into my nostrils, but the sweet smell of terra cotta was gone.

"I don't know," Bessie said, squeezing my hand. "You'll just have to wait and see."

WHILE MOTHER and the Kingpin consummated their
marriage that night in Mother's bedroom, I rolled the giant
bowling ball out of my bedroom and down the hall. The
clay had hardened and was cracked, the finger holes had
become more oval than round. The night air had been too
cool, the breeze coming through the window had caused it
to dry unevenly, the side facing the window sagged and
pocked with tiny air holes. I considered glazing it with
pink shoe polish to cover up its imperfections, but thought
it was better to leave it untouched, for the smell of raw clay
to linger when you pressed your nose against it.

I could hear the Kingpin shouting, Mother's high-pitched
moans. "Oh, Stan, Stan," she called like a stage actress. Stan
let out a low sustained moan, a note of frenzied lovemaking.
For a minute I half-expected my father to emerge from the
bedroom in his briefs, red-faced and screaming.

"Making art is like making love to the self," he once
wrote in a note to Mother which he slipped under the
basement door when he would no longer come out for fear
of the chainsaw men coming for all of us. Of course art had
never been enough for Mother, which was why I believed
she now made love to the Kingpin.

Quietly I rolled the ball outside their door and took out
one of the chainsaw men that I'd found in Mother's drawer. With the tip of the chainsaw I scratched the words, *To
Your New Life, In the Name of Art* underneath Mother's
name.

When the sounds finally died down, I tiptoed back to
my bedroom and fell asleep with the lights on.

Mother's screams woke me the next morning. She was
ranting and raving, the Kingpin mumbling for her to calm
down. I heard a splash of water and then the cracking of
the clay bowling ball as she smashed it to pieces.

"How could you, Frances?" she screamed. "How could you think I would like a piece of clay?"

I shoved my head under the pillow and closed my eyes. I kept them closed, even when she banged on the door and screamed my name, louder and louder like a hysteric. For a minute I felt like a little girl again, hiding under the pillow and listening to the screams. "The chainsaw men are coming, the chainsaw men are coming!" I could almost hear my father shout. I opened my eyes and thought I saw his large fleshy body move past my window, the flesh jiggling over the waistband of a pair of spanking new briefs. For just that moment, it was as if I'd brought him back.

CHAPTER THREE

While I'm signing books a woman tells me that it is impossible to cut a pair of tusks with a chainsaw. The ivory resists, she says, flies up in your face and shoots shards into your eyes. You'd wish you'd been born blind, instead of haunting aquariums with a pen in your pocket, wishing you could live underwater.

MY FATHER SOLD HIS FIRST CHAINSAW MAN, aptly titled *Man with Chainsaw*, to a small gallery in New York when I was ten. It was the kind of gallery where people often springboarded to bigger and better things, the owner said. He wore a green velvet jacket and a goatee. Together he and my father sat in the living room drinking wine and laughing. Mother stayed on the front stoop drinking coffee and watching the cars pass by while I sat huddled by the stairs listening and peeking in at them.

Soon he was being interviewed by *Modern Sculpture* for a piece devoted to emerging artists. My father agreed to wear a proper shirt for the interviewer's visit but refused to put on a pair of pants. His briefs would soon become his trademark, what the reviewers would call "a nakedness of the soul." To Mother, they were a constant reminder of the way her life had been stripped away. For me they'd become everything, even moved into my dreams at night.

"I am threadbare and weary," she would say loudly from the front porch. It was her favorite refrain.

At the time I thought of my father's underpants as an open secret. We weren't supposed to look at them, yet there they were day after day, plain as the nose on your face. My father poured wine for the interviewer and spoke in a loud voice about how the man with the chainsaw had come to him in a dream. He held the chainsaw in the air as if waving a flag, my father said, and inched closer to the bed.

"I see him there in the corner of my eye, the blades spinning beneath his hands. There is no one in the room to help me. He comes closer, inch by inch, until he stands beside my bed and aims the chainsaw at my throat. I open my mouth to scream, but no sound comes. He lowers the chainsaw bit by bit, and then I wake up, just before the blood starts to spurt."

He laughed then and rubbed his hands over the clay figure, up and down over the man's body. I hugged my knees to my chest and felt my breath coming faster and faster. His briefs were ringed with blotches of terra cotta, holes the size of nickels in the seams.

"It's a happening," the interviewer said, and I felt a shiver go through me. My father turned and saw me peeking out from behind the stairs. He winked at me and flashed his teeth.

"My daughter Frances," he said with a gleam in his eye, "has seen chainsaws first hand. She knows art when she sees it."

"One of the most interesting artists to appear in recent years is Morton Fisk, a sculptor whose terra cotta figures, Men With Chainsaws, *clearly suggest a symbolic correlation with twentieth century violence. The figures, miniature plastic earth reliefs*

with aluminum chainsaws in their hands, personify the self-destructive impulses of modern man. The arms of the figures are long and fragile when contrasted with the thickness of the body and base, as if the magnitude of the violent instruments of society has weighed down the very soul of man. In Fisk's work one sees the scope of an artist profoundly disturbed by mainstream society's embrace of self-destruction.

Fisk's work exploits the conventional notion of the "angry young man" to encompass the rage which modern man experiences in the face of the breakdown of society. The painstaking detail of the chainsaws (in contrast with the faceless plastic earth figures) underlines both the ways in which violence is interwoven with civilization and the means by which humanity is forced to stand stoically by while modern society seeks to destroy itself through its own violent tendencies. Fisk's Men With Chainsaws *suggest both the hope of man's harnessing of his sadistic impulses and the paradoxical futility of society's attempts to suppress violence, even in its most basic forms."*

WHEN THE MAN was gone my father went back to work, slapping and twisting the clay into shape. He began with a thick ball of clay the size of his fist for the torso which clung to the armature to keep the figure at a standing position. Within minutes, almost without seeming to move his hands, hips appeared, and then a long roll of clay which eventually became the legs. He laughed while he spritzed the clay with a spray bottle, grunted as he cut the formation of the chainsaw from a sheet of aluminum with tin-snips. When the figures were dry he fired and then glazed them with everyday household items—shoe polish, wood varnish, Mother's Mop-n-Glo. The reviewers later lauded him for this, for what they felt was his refusal to embrace elitism and his determination to bring art to the common man. Finally, when the figures became cool to the touch, he slipped the handle of the chainsaws into the small openings left in their fists, the metal gliding between the thumb and forefinger that resembled a gesture of "okay."

After he became famous I could no longer watch him work and had to content myself instead with the heat coming from the kiln in the basement where he fired the men at all hours of the night. At times the house became stifling and Mother would strip the covers off to cool me down, waiting for me to fall asleep, her coffee breath sweet on my face.

Soon there were men from museums coming to the house at all hours of the day and night. Gallery owners and interviewers all wanted a piece of him, to get close to the frenzied workings of an artistic mind. My father would scream in a state of ecstasy as each of the new chainsaw men appeared to him. Later when the art collectors and gallery owners came to the house to talk with him while he ate bars of chocolate, he grew increasingly morose. Mother busied herself with preparing hors d'oeuvres and pouring drinks for the men while I sat in my best party dress and crossed my legs like a young lady.

"Sit up straight, Frances," Mother would say, "your father's patrons are coming."

She loved the attention back then, loved the feel of the word "patron" on her lips. She said it whenever she had the chance, puckering her lips for the "p" sound and letting the hiss of the "s" drag on the end. It was all so new to her—the flirtation, men kissing her hand and telling her what a genius her husband was, how fortunate she must feel. Oh, yes, she agreed, Morton was a genius. She relished the creative life. She smoked cigarettes and talked about the rain in a breathy voice. But when the patrons were gone she went back to the porch to sit in the dark drinking coffee and watching the headlights go by. My father would pace the floor in his briefs, cursing under his breath. Sometimes the visions wouldn't come and he was left in a state of despair, choking down pieces of bread while waiting for the next vision.

"They've deserted me," he'd say. He'd pound the clay with his fists and weep. Once he hooked his thumbs in the waistband of his briefs and tore them away in one fluid motion. Naked, he stood there in the living room, his stomach hanging low, his whole body matted with red fingerprints.

"For God's sake, Morton," Mother said under her breath, throwing a blanket over him, "this is no way for Frances to live."

And yet it was the only life I knew. At night after Mother was asleep I would tiptoe to my father's workroom and watch his hands mold the clay, fingers pinching, his eyes closed, the flesh of his neck jiggling with the movement of his arms. When I couldn't stay awake any longer, I tried to fall asleep with that image in mind, my father's hulking back moving under the light, the fingers curving as if they had a mind of their own. Nothing else, I thought, could ever match that kind of beauty.

WHEN HIS FIRST major review appeared in *The New York Times*, everything changed. We moved to a large house— the house that he would die in—and my father no longer worked where anyone could see him. His was a private vision, he said, and having the world read about it was more than he could bear. He moved his kiln down to the basement and sealed himself in. The chainsaw men were coming all the time now, he said, but only when he was alone.

The recent exhibit of the work of Morton Fisk at the MOMA *exemplifies the existential despair experienced by today's major artists. His* Men With Chainsaws *is the brilliant embodiment of the individual in conflict with itself and the world in which he lives. The mixed media creation of plastic earth figures with welded metallic chainsaws evokes the manic paranoia of Dali, preoccupation with the self, and a narcissistic impulse driven to such heights as to seek to destroy itself. Fisk is a man of vision, an artist profoundly in touch with the unconscious mind, the id personified, the chainsaw a tool designed both to protect and destroy the chaotic world the artist seeks desperately to order.*

For Fisk, the Men With Chainsaws *series constitutes the transient state of the imagination. The earthy terra cotta figure (which is glazed with household cleaners to underline the importance of simplicity in a complex world) combined with the brashness of the aluminum saw symbolizes society's continuous struggle to reconcile the infinite world of the imagination with the banality of the trivial world. The exhibit at the* MOMA: Men With Chainsaws, Fifth Series *is further evidence of this unresolved societal conflict. In Fisk's work, the chainsaw both dwarfs the often crudely depicted figures and yet acts as a constant against which to measure its size, each series seeking to amplify the effect of the chainsaw as symbolic of the unwieldiness of art in everyday life. Each* Man With Chainsaw *is reduced in size and stature, creating the effect of order in a chaotic world, the need for the human mind to reduce concepts to smaller components. With the sufficient reduction of the figures, one can begin to appreciate the complexity of a man of Fisk's incomparable vision in the totality of his work.*

The recent series combines the raw featureless faces of the men themselves with the intricacies of the aluminum chainsaws. The most prominent features of the figures themselves are the bases, oval platforms upon which the feet of the sculptures rest.

Each toe is clearly delineated and elongated, suggesting the need to find one's footing in an expanding universe. The figures' inverse graduation in size, emphasized by the fixed size and workmanship of the chainsaws, underlines the continuous need for reduction of broader concepts in the minds of today's work-ing class. The Man With Chainsaw *is both artist and Every-man seeking survival in a violent society.*

Artist and Everyman. The banality of the everyday world. How was it that my father had come upon these ideas? Mother said that art was something we would never under-stand. He moved down to the basement and we were left to ourselves to wonder what all of this meant. With him sealed away beneath us, Mother seemed more at ease. We rode bicycles down the residential streets and played hop-scotch in the rain. Anything to avoid the screams. They came more and more frequently, all through the night and into the early morning hours. More than screams, they were cackles really. When I asked her why he screamed that way, Mother would only say that my father had an overactive mind and dreamed more than the average person.

"He's dreaming when they come to him," she'd say, pat-ting my hand more for her own reassurance than for mine. "And when he wakes up, he can do nothing but sculpt."

More than anything I longed to watch him work. I didn't know what I'd done to warrant my exile from his studio. I missed watching while he molded his men, hooking wads of terra cotta on to armatures and letting them harden in the cool air. I didn't know why he'd deserted me, why he never came upstairs to let me feed him pieces of cake. Mother said I was better off not seeing him, that I would understand when I was older that my father's torment was not something a daughter should see. And yet I would wait at the basement door until the newest figure appeared. He slipped them out the door and lined them up on cooling racks, one by one, like soldiers.

THE WEIGHT GAIN started when he surrendered his entire life to his art. Even a task as simple as waiting for his next meal became too tedious for him. Art required total surrender, he said. Scheduled meals and an ordered life were luxuries an artist could ill afford. He told Mother that we'd all be better off the sooner we realized that normal life had nothing to offer, that soon enough we'd all be dead and unless we took action, we would have nothing to show for it but a thin corpse. Life was a cheat, he said, unless you sucked it dry. All society had done was to try to control man's most natural impulse by inventing the absurd notion of three meals a day.

"I'll eat when and as often as I want to," he said, and shoved wedges of cheese into his mouth until his cheeks bulged.

He stopped coming to meals because they were another of society's conventions imposed upon the artist. He'd eat when he had to and would keep eating until he felt himself satisfied. There was no telling when that might be. Sometimes he ate nonstop for days at a time, banging on the door until he'd helped himself to everything in the refrigerator but the ketchup bottles. At meal times I delivered heaping plates of meats and puddings to him, a carton of milk for added strength. Occasionally he refrained from using the toilet, preferring instead to piss on the floor or into a jar. His art was making lots of money then, and the gallery owners urged Mother to indulge him.

"Let him do what he wants," they said, "and you'll have all the money you need to make you happy. What *does* make you happy, Arlene?"

They asked her this question for an article about the para-
dox of my father's disdain for convention while embracing
middle America by sculpting angry men with chainsaws.

"Something simple," she said, "like maybe bowling."

The quote had appeared on the front page of a major art
magazine. I'd never been more mortified.

Every day she'd get down on her hands and knees and
scrub the floors with a toothbrush dipped in paste wax.
When I told her I didn't see any clay on the floors, she said
I wasn't looking hard enough.

"Open your eyes, Frances," she snapped. "The clay is
everywhere."

It became a daily routine. Together we would fill the bathtub with water and bring buckets into the kitchen, where we
poured sudsy water over the white ceramic tile. She wiped
the furniture and lamps, even our clothes, with a sopping
sponge. Everywhere you looked the water hung in thick
drops, soaking. There was nowhere you could sit to escape it.

One day my father opened the basement door and let
loose a piercing scream. Mother and I jumped up from the
kitchen floor, the toothbrushes scattered in every direction.
I ran ahead of her and stopped short. It had been weeks
since I'd seen him, and I gasped out loud when I looked
down at him standing there in his briefs. His hair was
weighted down with grease, blotches of clay stuck along
the length of his arms and over his bare chest. When he
opened his mouth to scream, the clay even covered his
teeth. They were gray and mottled with film.

"Here they come," he screamed, reaching his arms out as
if to grab me. I stood against the bannister, not sure
whether to run and help him or turn the other way. My feet
froze on the stairs. He opened his eyes wide and looked
straight through me. "I've got no way out," he said, and

then slammed the door so hard that some of Mother's china fell from the shelves in the living room.

Neither of us said anything. Mother took my hand and led me back to the kitchen where we stood facing each other, our eyes averted. She held on to me and poured the bucket of water over both of our heads, drenching us as we stood between the sink and the stove. The water was warm as it ran down our chins, dripping down the front of my dress. I opened my eyes and watched Mother through the tunnel of water while my father screamed and screamed.

"Those men will be the death of him," she said.

I wrung out the front of my soaking dress. I wanted to run to the basement door, bang on it, and yell down the stairs, ask him what it felt like to live with a head full of men trying to kill him with chainsaws. Why art meant giving up toilets and running around in his underpants. But I knew Mother would never allow that. She gripped my hand and kept on pouring until we were both too soaked to move.

WE COMMUNICATED with him only through notes. *Accountant says CD's due at end of month,* Mother wrote. *Guggenheim sends letter of thanks. Frances will be fourteen next week. This is not a life.*

Late one night when I delivered his supper, I sat down on the stairs and scribbled a note on a napkin.

> *Dear Dad,*
>
> *Do you miss having meals at the table? If Mother stops cleaning, will you come upstairs and live with us again? Why do the chainsaw men keep getting smaller?*
>
> *Love,*
> *Frances*

I sat on the steps for hours waiting for answers that never came. Mother scrubbed the floors in the hallway and sang lullabies to herself in a sad voice. She must have seen me sitting there on the steps, but she never looked at me or bothered to call my name to see where I might be. It seemed I'd vanished for her as much as my father had, and that she was letting us both float away as if we'd never been there in the first place. As I watched her waxing and buffing the floors, I realized that Mother had left me, just as my father had. There seemed to be nothing that would bring her back from her life of cleaning.

ONCE BESSIE moved in with us we had some hope. A calm came over Mother with Bessie there to help her. For the first time that I could remember, she had a sense of communion in her life. When she and Bessie washed the floors or scrubbed the bathtub, Mother would even smile to herself. She let me play checkers with her out on the porch and asked Bessie to teach her to French braid my hair. Once in a while she still winced when a new chain-saw man appeared on the basement steps, but for the most part she seemed content, as if she'd forgotten my father completely.

The first thing Bessie did was to alert Mother to the fact that my father hadn't bathed in nearly a year. There was no sense in a grown man living in such filth, Bessie said, art or no art. She pinched her nose with a clothespin and said we had to get him out of the basement before he drove us out of our own home. It wouldn't matter how much they cleaned, she said, if my father stunk till Kingdom come. We'd become so used to the smell of his rot and the clay melding into one that the odor had become a part of our daily life, as natural as breathing.

"He needs a good cleaning," Bessie said. "We have to get him into the tub."

On this subject Mother and Bessie were of one mind. They both believed in cleanliness above all else. There was nothing in life that couldn't be cured with a scrub brush and a bar of soap. When Bessie was feeling low, all she had to do was scrub her cheeks with Ivory and pat them dry with a clean towel.

We worked on schemes for a week before finally coming up with a plan to lure him into the tub. I carried notes from Mother on his dinner tray every night. In black magic marker she wrote, *What you do to yourself is one thing, but the smell is quite another. A bath is not too much to ask.* And finally, *This stench must end.*

I tucked the notes under the plate of bread or between wedges of cheese. Each night there were five or six new figures wrapped in damp cloth waiting for me outside the basement door.

Dad,

Bessie is here now. You would like her. She says it's not healthy to eat so much. They say you need to use soap and water, that it's important to be clean. Won't you have a bath? It would make us all so happy.

Love,
Frances

There was no response.

Bessie found him several days later. He lay face down on the bathroom floor with his arm curved over the edge of the tub. His briefs were reduced to shreds of cotton that barely covered his privates. The water was filled to the brim, high enough that his fingers were gently submerged.

Mother called the funeral home and hugged me tightly against her breast. "I want to see his face," I told her, but she said it was best that I remember him the way he had been before the chainsaw men had come.

"You don't want to see him like that, honey," Bessie said. "Sometimes it's better not to see."

The men from the funeral parlor rolled a long brown bag on a stretcher and locked the door behind them. I imagined them cutting the shreds of his briefs and wrapping him in a clean white sheet. I leaned against the door and heard the soft splash of water, the suction of his body as they peeled him off the floor. I banged and banged for them to let me in, but the water drowned out my voice and I was left sitting against the door, waiting to say good-bye. When Mother wasn't looking I sat on the floor and ran my finger along the blade of one of his chainsaw men, the teeth tearing through my skin. I let the blood run along my palm and down the length of my arm. They opened the door and wheeled him outside into the sunshine, his body zipped into the long brown bag. I stood there in the driveway as the station wagon pulled away with my father's body. Blood dripped down the curve of my arm and splattered over the asphalt. The longer I stood there, the bloodier my arm became. Later, when the stains became caked in my hand, I refused to wipe them away.

CHAPTER FOUR

*It is the plight of all women to think we need something
large and wrinkled in our lives to give us a sense of worth,
Bessie says. To tell us their secrets and stab us full of ivory
charm. This is what women tell each other at aquariums,
she says. They bowl to try to forget.*

THE DAY WE MOVED, THE KINGPIN STOOD IN THE
bedroom doorway and flashed me a smile. His
hands were shoved inside his pockets, thumbs
twirling.

"You'll be bowling before you know it," he said, shifting
his weight from one hip to the other. "It may not be art, but
it gets in your blood just the same."

I smiled at him and put down my dust pan. I took a long
look at his hips, searching in vain for underwear lines.
Without the wingtips and the smell of bowling balls on his
hands, I thought, the Kingpin wouldn't be half bad.

"Yes, I guess it does," I said, because I could think of
nothing else.

The Kingpin nodded. We seemed to understand each
other as best we could. He must have sensed the disap-
pointment I felt in moving from a genius to a bowler in the
long spectrum of father figures. And though I didn't know

what kind of life the Kingpin had before he'd met Mother, I was sure he hadn't banked on a stepdaughter who liked to make enormous clay bowling balls for her mother. Still, we each seemed to have accepted that this was how it was to be, for better or worse. We might have had different dreams, but this was the way life had turned out for us.

I was about to say that I was looking forward to Florida, which of course was a lie because it pained me to leave my father's house, though I thought the Kingpin might have liked to hear it.

I said silent good-bye's to each one of the rooms, pausing at the door to the bathroom where Bessie had found him dead that day, his heavy weight splayed over the floor. Part of me wanted to cry, but I promised myself that I wouldn't. I lay a hand on the outside of the bathroom door and lowered my head, but couldn't bring myself to open it. Instead I walked across the kitchen floor and sat there on the cold tile, leaned my head against the basement door and thought of all the times I'd felt the warmth of his kiln from there. On nights when I couldn't sleep, I'd steal down the steps and press my face against the door to listen to the firing, drawing comfort from the heat on my face and the constant clicking of his tinsnips. How quiet it was when he was working, when he was filled with the intoxication of his vision. But the quiet never seemed to last very long and I'd be jolted back to bed by the ache in his voice, the screams that seemed to shake the foundation.

"Are you ready to go?" Bessie asked.

She walked down the steps and sat with me. I nodded and leaned my head on her shoulder, feeling her soft breath on my hair. Once I'd overheard Bessie telling Mother about her daughter who had drowned at high tide, how difficult it had been to forgive herself for not having saved her, even though she wasn't there when it happened. I knew enough never to ask questions about it, but I also knew that Bessie understood grief, how it felt to be helpless in the face of death. I wondered if she was nervous about moving to the beach, if the water all around her would serve as a constant reminder. I was certainly nervous about it, since my father had died on his way to the bathtub, and none of us had been able to save him. Of course I could say none of this to Bessie. Some things were just unsayable.

I lifted my head and took a deep breath. Bessie squeezed my hand.

"Sometimes leaving a place brings you back even more," she said. She pressed both of her hands to my cheeks and stared at me, and I felt the tears well up, thought of my father in his briefs with water running down his face.

"But I don't want to go," I said, and Bessie nodded, pulled me up to my feet, and led me across the kitchen floor to the front hall. I turned back only once to look at the sealed door and then snapped my head forward again.

THE KINGPIN'S HOUSE was surrounded by the beach on all sides. On one side a large sun deck wrapped itself around half of the house, on the other a spiral staircase wound its way down to the sand. Mother and the Kingpin ran straight for the water and splashed each other, Mother's lacy bra showing through her gauze blouse. When they thought I wasn't looking the Kingpin grabbed her around the waist and pressed his hips against her. I turned my back to Mother's squeals of pleasure.

It rained for the first three days in Florida. I didn't mind, since I was busy arranging my room, clearing out the boxes and setting my father's sculptures on tables and book-shelves above my bed. Although sometimes it pained me even to look at them, I still felt they were my protectors. With the chainsaw men around me, I hoped I could keep the Kingpin at bay.

Most of the Kingpin's furniture had a Floridian coolness about it—futons draped in sprays of corals and sea foam greens, bleached wood shelves cluttered with bowling trophies. Above the turquoise leather sectional hung life-size portraits of Earl Anthony and Dick Weber, the two greatest bowlers who had ever lived, according to what the Kingpin had told me. Earl looked straight at the camera in his white bowling shirt with his name stenciled in burgundy letters; Dick held a Mona Lisa smile, his lips turned up at the edges. Apparently the Kingpin had met them in their prime and convinced them to sit for portraits in one of his bowling alleys. It was, he said, his finest hour.

"The first time I met Earl Anthony," he said, stepping back from the portrait to lay his cowboy hat on the arm of the sofa, "he was about to become the first bowler to make a million bucks. I'll never forget the way he walked past the crowd, almost like he didn't see us there, like his mind was already focused on the pins. When he stooped down to pick up his ball, I leaned forward and forced myself to say it."

I stared into Earl's touched-up blue eyes, at the part in his dirty blond hair that revealed the whitish hint of scalp. The Kingpin touched me lightly on the arm, his fingers brushing my elbow as if to give me my cue to speak.

"What did you say?" I said, inching away from him. With my face tilted at an angle I could almost feel their eyes on me, the deep blue of Earl Anthony's gaze and Dick Weber's hard stare.

"I said," the Kingpin whispered, closing his eyes as he leaned forward, "'Good Luck, Earl.'"

Of course, I thought as I turned away from him, leaving him to revel in the memory. What else could you say to a bowler?

THE FIRST THING Mother did was to hang her wedding portrait between the photos of Dick and Earl. She had the photo enlarged and framed in blond wood, a twenty by twenty-eight inch mural of the four of us in our satin and lace. We'd never had family portraits taken when my father was alive, even before he was famous. The walls had always been bare. Photos of me as an infant were kept in an album with yellowed pages and cracks in the binding. We knew who we were, Mother had always said. There was no need to advertise. But now she wanted nothing more than to have herself and the Kingpin sandwiched between the pros. It was more than she'd hoped for.

"We're a real family now," she said, as she balanced the wire brace on the nail she'd hammered in herself.

There was nothing I could think of to say in reply. When she wasn't looking I tilted the photos of Earl and Dick a quarter of an inch to the right. All that mattered to Mother was that we were all together there on the wall. What difference would it make to her that all three portraits were crooked?

Mother had been looking forward to the beach and to having her blonde hair streaked from the sun, but she and Bessie busied themselves with cleaning before anything else could be done. The dustballs under the beds and wads of hair in the tub were evidence that the Kingpin hadn't been much of a housekeeper before Mother came into his life. But she didn't seem to mind. She bustled around the house with a sponge and a smile, kissing the Kingpin every chance she had.

"The place is filthy," Bessie whispered to her while they were scrubbing out the mold in one of the bathtubs. Given my father's history, Bessie always made sure that all the bathtubs were spotless.

"So what if it is?" Mother said with a toss of her head. "At least it isn't from clay."

Mother had agreed to give me the remaining chainsaw men as long as they were confined to my bedroom. If she ever saw one on the stairwell, or caught a glimpse of the metal teeth, then all bets were off. I agreed to this whole-heartedly. She'd given up on my father a long time ago—now I could have him all to myself.

We all went to bed early the first night. Mother and the Kingpin were across the hall and Bessie's room was right next to mine. The move had exhausted us. I pressed my ear to the door to hear Bessie snoring. There was nothing more comforting than the dry rumble of her breath, the rhythm of her snores.

I took my clothes off and rolled them in a ball by the side of the bed. Slowly I eased myself between the sheets, the coolness soothing the indentations where the elastic seam of my panties had dug into my flesh. The venetian blinds were turned down, a hint of light coming through the slats. I pressed my hands into the flatness of my belly and lower, swirling my hips against the sheets. I thought of that night on the lawn with Frank, the way he'd pressed against me, the sheen of his skin under the moonlight. The warm feel of cotton briefs against the palm of my hand, the stabbing of desire. My fingers moved deeper, circling the flesh, as I closed my eyes against the light from the blinds. I thought of the splash of my father's piss hitting the lawn and gasped.

Someone tapped at the door. I pulled my hands up to my sides and tightened the sheets around me.

"Frances," the Kingpin said, "if there's anything you need . . ."

I coughed deep in my throat and rolled over on my side, bringing my knees up into a ball.

"I'm fine," I said. "I don't need anything."

After a minute I heard his footsteps heading down the hallway, the clicking of a locked door. I opened my eyes and watched the trees form shadows on the blinds. The tears came quickly, rolling down into my open mouth. I didn't know why I was crying really, but the feeling gripped me in the chest and stayed there. With the back of my hand I wiped away the tears and closed my eyes to keep the light out, so I could no longer see the blinds.

THE KINGPIN intended to unveil his new family at the grand opening of his newest bowling alley. I didn't want to go, but Bessie said it was best not to put up a fight, that the sooner I accepted the Kingpin, the better it was for all concerned. She had reservations about him, she said, but she was thrilled to see that she'd been right about Mother, that bowling was just what she'd needed.

"As long as Arlene is happy," she said, "then we've got to do our best by her."

The Kingpin insisted that we wear our wedding clothes to show the people of Sarasota what a fine family he'd gotten for himself. This was the largest alley that had ever been built in Florida, he said, and what better way to usher it in than with all of us decked out to the nines. Apparently it was not uncommon in Florida for people to wear formal wear to bowling alleys, Mother said. We were just following tradition.

The whole idea was ludicrous, Bessie agreed, but the opening of a bowling alley was the largest kind of celebration the Kingpin knew of. I agreed to play along, despite myself.

I hoped the bowling alley at least had some decent pizza.

Bessie stood in the hallway in her pink satin and rolled her eyes. Mother had on her bridal dress and the Kingpin wore a brand new pair of wingtips. They were all decked out and waiting for me while I dug through my closet to look for my dress.

"I can't find it," I called to Mother. The closet was full of chainsaw men and old reviews. In the back of the closet I'd tossed whatever clothes I'd had in my suitcase, not much caring what I'd be wearing once I left my father's house. In this hurried state I'd forgotten my bras and panties.

I heard Mother mutter something under her breath, the click of her high heels over the linoleum floor. She stood in the doorway with her hands on her hips, keeping her eyes on me at all times, careful not to turn her head to see the hundreds of chainsaw men positioned all over the room. If she managed to see them in her peripheral vision, she never let on.

"Is there nothing you won't do," she said with tears in her eyes, "to thwart every chance we have for a better life?"

I turned my back to her and kept digging in the closet. It was not my idea of a better life, I wanted to say, to wear a lace gown to a bowling alley and fawn over the Kingpin. To hoard my father's artwork in a bedroom when it should be out for all the world to see. To live right on the ocean when my father had died in the tub. But I kept all this to myself. I was supposed to suffer in silence. That was one of the things Mother had taught me.

I felt a ball of lace at the bottom of the closet and yanked.

"Here it is," I said, pulling it up from under the boxes and holding it up in the air for Mother to see.

Mother's eyes were blank when I finally looked at her and then down at the dress. The pink lace was stained with clay, the edges torn apart by chainsaws. All of the threads had come loose and hung down in a mound of string weighted down in lumps of dried terra cotta.

"I'm sorry," I said, and truly I was, but I knew that wasn't going to be enough.

WE ARRIVED at the bowling alley at nearly nine o'clock, just in time, the Kingpin said, for the family league. Bowling had a tendency to bring families together, he said, giving Mother a secret smile. She beamed at him and reached over to touch me lightly on the arm, but I walked ahead with Bessie and pretended not to notice.

The bowling alley was huge, a sprawling red building with "STAN's 50" flashing in purple neon lights. When we got closer to the front door, a dozen flashbulbs went off in our faces. The press was everywhere, thrusting their microphones at the Kingpin in hope of a comment. But the Kingpin just smiled and held Mother's hand in both of his. I hid behind Bessie to shield my eyes from the flash.

"Just goes to show what some people will do for a news story," I whispered to Bessie, and she covered her mouth to keep from laughing.

"Turn this way, Stan," the reporters called. "Let's have a look at the missus." And finally, a lone voice above the crowd, "Show us your ball!"

Everyone laughed then, and the Kingpin murmured that he'd left his ball at home, but that certainly there would be no shortage of balls at this alley.

"And you can quote me on that," he said.

He turned and raised his cowboy hat to the crowd. The cheers were deafening. I looked over at Mother, and for a minute our eyes locked as we both remembered the many times reporters had camped outside the house during my father's latest exhibits to catch a glimpse of him with his face pressed up against the basement window, sometimes sneaking out into the front yard and yelling obscenities, a chainsaw man tucked in the waistband of his briefs. This was certainly not the kind of fame we were used to.

We walked into the alley together, Mother and the Kingpin in front, Bessie behind them and me bringing up the rear. In the Florida bowling world, no one was bigger than the Kingpin. Everyone applauded as we headed single file toward the front desk. We stood under the glare of the fluorescent lights—the Kingpin in his tux and wingtips, Mother in her chiffon, Bessie in pink satin, and I, braless in a T-shirt and denim skirt with no panties underneath, a pair of tired loafers on my feet. The crowd gathered around us and applauded, their eyes moving over Mother while they hooted and whistled. I tried to stay behind Bessie where no one could see me, but she pulled me next to her and wrapped her arm around me.

"Look at all those bowling balls!" Mother shrieked.

It was true. I'd never imagined there could be as many bowling balls as I saw there that night. Piles of them stood in every corner, barrels with the Kingpin's and Mother's names on them, red balls on the floor to form an enormous heart in the middle of the alley. White balls with wedding bells stenciled on them were set up in a pyramid directly across from the front desk. A man in a hooded sweatshirt held one over his head with a cowboy hat on it as a salute to the Kingpin. Everywhere you looked the shock of a bowling ball hit you in the face. There was no way to escape it.

The Kingpin walked to the front desk and grabbed the microphone. Bessie and I just stood there as people stared at us. A woman in a red T-shirt with the words "I Love Trouble" on it winked at Bessie and rocked her bowling ball in her arms. The Kingpin cleared his throat over the sound system and coughed a few times. Sweat ran down under the brim of his hat and hung in thick drops over his nose. My nipples hardened into points that threatened to poke through my thin cotton shirt. To hide them I folded my arms tightly over my chest. I stared down at my loafers and felt the air rush between my legs, my skirt swaying in the cool air. Without my panties to protect me, anything could happen. I prayed for the night to end.

"Ladies and gentlemen," the Kingpin announced in a booming voice I'd never heard before, "here, at the greatest alley in the world, is my new family."

The applause rang out through the alley, the sound of balls whizzing down lanes and the crashing of pins. I reached for Bessie's hand and held on to it.

The Kingpin sidled over to Bessie and me with his arm still around Mother. Would he ever let go, I wondered, now that he had her down in Florida among his bowling alleys? Mother pressed a nervous hand to her chignon and flashed her teeth at him.

"This is my wife Arlene," he said. "My cup runneth over."

The smell of pizza was faint at first, but then it got stronger, the heat from the ovens hitting me in waves. I felt my mouth water, a shaking in my legs. For the next few minutes I heard nothing. The bowling alley had suddenly come to a standstill and I was alone, drowning in a sea of bowling balls. Sweat ran down my back and formed pools beneath my breasts. Hundreds of balls kept spinning, spinning, as the smell of the pizza overtook me.

"And this is my stepdaughter Frances," I heard, and the next thing I knew I was down, a quick surge of heat and then the cold blast of concrete in the face as I hit the ground.

WHEN I CAME TO, Bessie was wiping my forehead with a cool cloth, her brown hand soothing, the satin of her sleeve against my face. She whispered to someone crouched next to her, though I couldn't see who it was. I sniffed deeply, but smelled only Bessie's perfume and faint perspiration.

"What happened?" I asked. Bile welled up in the back of my throat, the dust of bowling balls drifting up my nose.

"Too much excitement, sugar," Bessie said.

A hand reached around and lifted a white paper cup to my lips. I felt it support the back of my neck as I sipped from the cup, the cool water moving down my throat. It was a man's hand, I could tell that much from the wiry hairs and the earthy smell of the palm.

"Take shallow breaths when there's pizza around," the voice said, a deep voice, soft, like he was telling some kind of secret. "Always drink lots of fluids in a bowling alley," and then, in a breathless whisper, "And never, never go without underwear."

I drank the rest of the water and tried to sit up. "Easy honey," Bessie said, and then Mother was on me, wrapping her chiffon arms around my head. A lacquered tendril stabbed me in the eye, and for a minute I couldn't see. I blinked back the tears, trying to focus. They pulled me to my feet and when I stood up, the voice was gone. The bowling alley was silent as we made our way out the door.

Outside I took deep breaths until my vision became clear again. The air was cool on my arms. I could still hear the pins crashing inside. I suggested that Bessie take me home while Mother and the Kingpin went on with the grand opening party, but Mother wouldn't hear of it. She sat in the back seat with Bessie and me while the Kingpin drove in silence. I laid my head against the warmth of Bessie's pink satin as Mother held my hand and sniffled. All the way home I thought about the earthy hand holding the cup to my lips, the softness of that voice. I wondered how he'd known that I wasn't wearing any underwear, that the smell of pizza had left me weak in the knees. And how he'd known that all those bowling balls would prove too much for me, that the sight of whirling rubber would fill up my head and send me gasping for air, face down on the concrete.

FOR A WEEK Mother insisted I stay in bed while Bessie delivered bowls of soup and relayed messages of love from Mother. After her initial visit to my bedroom while I was looking for the dress, Mother had vowed not to set foot in there again. Seeing the chainsaw men stirred up in her the thickness of my father's memory. She'd no longer keep me from his art, she said, but she wouldn't be a part of it either, especially in the Kingpin's house. She wouldn't risk losing his bowling balls for anything.

While I lay in my room I felt a sense of déjà vu hanging in the air all around us. I remembered taking down trays of food to my father's room and leaving them at the bottom of the basement steps. Two or three times a day I descended the staircase with a tray of meatloaf and bowls of mashed potatoes, a bottle of milk and bars of chocolate. Art had set within him an insatiable appetite. Every night I'd slide a note under the door on a napkin which I secretly pressed with a kiss of Mother's lipstick. Now here I was, sick from too many bowling balls, with Mother sliding notes under my door. Only art had all but abandoned me and I had no appetite for anything but pizza. When I asked if we could order one, Mother said that I could have soup and crackers only.

"All the fat in that cheese," she told Bessie. "It could kill her."

Bessie came in twice a day for an update on my condition and to encourage me to get back on my feet. She brought me a sensible cotton bra and packages of new panties in every color of the rainbow—a belated birthday gift, she said. Two sizes too small, just the way I liked them. They were wrapped in cellophane, pinks and yellows glaring out at me from under the price tags. I tried on the bra and a new pair of French cut yellow panties and stood at the mirror looking hard at my body. My breasts were long and pointed beneath the smooth cotton cups, patches of brownish hair poked through the elastic trim around my groin. I thought of asking Bessie if she thought I looked like my father, but with my wiry hair and clear blue eyes I saw Mother staring me in the face. My skin was as smooth as a bowling ball.

Bessie arranged the chainsaw men on the shelf over my head and fluffed my pillows. She said she'd overheard the Kingpin and Mother talking about my fainting spell in the kitchen one night and that the Kingpin was riddled with guilt.

"Maybe Florida won't agree with her," he'd said. "Maybe she's not over her grief."

Bessie held my hand as she told me this and nodded slowly with her eyes closed, as if this were some profound truth. I felt a shiver go through me, all the way down to the base of my spine. The tears caught in my throat. She patted my hair and kissed me on the cheek, leaving me a plate of Oreos and a tall glass of milk. Grief was everywhere I looked.

"You get yourself better," she said, "and we'll sneak off to the aquarium."

The sharks. I'd almost forgotten about them. Their rows of jagged teeth and impenetrable eyes. I hadn't touched a ball of clay in weeks. I smiled at Bessie as she closed the door behind her, but my heart wasn't in it. With one hand I smoothed the wrinkles in my new cotton panties, my fingers moving down over the bumpy thatch of hair. I moved my hand in circles, the way my father did when he sculpted, tried to dizzy myself with arousal. But no matter how hard I tried to make the feelings return, I felt no sense of joy at the prospect of seeing the sharks again.

CHAPTER FIVE

*Bowling is the great American lie, but pizza feeds
the soul.*

*This is what I hear when I'm alone watching shad-
ows dance on the venetian blinds. At first the voice is
like a dream, but then it is everywhere, booming
through bowling alleys, shaking the bedsprings. I hang
on until my fingers are raw and bleeding, until I'm
forced to let go . . .*

EVERY NIGHT WHILE I LAY IN BED I HEARD THEIR
lovemaking. It started with the slap of water from
their king-sized waterbed, rhythmic and slow at
first, then heavier, like the pounding of the surf outside my
window. I brought my knees up to my chest and held one
of the chainsaw men out in front of me like a sword. With
my head pressed against the pillows my chest tightened,
the elastic of my panties strangling my waist. Mother's
breath grew louder and more harsh, and I twisted my head
against the pillow, writhing with her breath until the
Kingpin's long and final scream. I squeezed a chainsaw
man with both hands until my palms bled, the metal teeth
leaving chinks in my hand. I wiped the blood on my underwear, smearing the perfect yellow with dark red blobs.

When it was over I closed my eyes and thought of
Mother in the next room with her legs splayed, the
chignon a tangle above her head. I wondered what she saw
in the Kingpin, how she could have once loved my father
and gone on to a man in wingtips who had nothing to offer
but portraits of aging bowling stars and bad teeth. Once
when I was eight or nine years old, I walked in on my
mother and father having sex. I'd been having some sort of
dream about a clay monster coming to get me—a frequent
and transparent dream of mine as a child—when I'd stum-
bled down the hallway to their bedroom and found the
door open a crack. I pushed it open and started to cry out
when I saw them. My hand flew over my mouth, catching
the air I'd expelled and sending it right back down my
throat.

They were on the floor, the flesh of my father's back rip-
pling in the moonlight. Mother's feet were high in the air
and she whimpered, low in her throat, like an animal. I
stood there rooted to the ground as I watched my father
pounding against her, his back a long shaking slab of flesh.
Before they could see me I ran out of the room, but when
I got into bed I could still hear the slap of their bodies,
kisses that smacked in the dark.

In later years when Mother looked back at the time
before art had overtaken my father, I sometimes caught her
sitting on the porch staring out at the headlights with a
yearning in her eyes. I wondered if she remembered that
night on the floor, the weight of him on her as their flesh
slapped with passion. Sometimes I thought of that night
when I was alone with my hands covered in clay or when
the chainsaw men cast shadows on my wall. Then I'd dip
my fingers in a glass of water the way Bessie had taught me
to. It would help me dream, she said, and usually it did, but

on those nights my eyes would fly open and I'd lie awake until my fingertips turned puckered and shriveled, the flesh of my fingers a terrible white.

AFTER A WEEK of convalescence, of being alone in my bedroom with only my father's men and the Kingpin's mating calls to distract me, I decided it was safe to leave the bedroom. I got out of bed and dusted all of my father's figures with a cheese cloth and tied my hair back with a red ribbon. The bowling balls that had been crashing in my head like a game of pinball had finally started to recede. The constant watering of my mouth had stopped, and I felt my hunger come back.

Mother and the Kingpin were sitting at the kitchen table eating granola cereal and drinking skim milk. Their faces were flushed with the sun and each other. I mumbled good morning and took my seat across from them, crossing my legs under the table. I had on two pairs of panties as an extra precaution. The Kingpin gave me a once-over and smiled into his bowl of granola.

"Well, well," Mother said with a cluck of her tongue as I sat down at the table and sipped at a glass of orange juice. She pressed her hand to my cheek and smiled. I smiled back and plucked a stray hair from the knot of her chignon. The Kingpin stared at me from the head of the table. Orange bubbles collided in my juice glass. I tried to erase the vision of him on top of Mother, his wingtips slapping with ecstasy. Now that I knew he'd seen my grief, I avoided his eyes at all cost.

Bessie served me a Western omelet and sat down beside me at the table. I could see she was grateful to have me back, that the strain of Mother and the Kingpin alone had taken its toll on her. There were deep circles around her brown eyes. The Kingpin sniffed at the wads of cheese oozing out of the sides of the omelet, but his better judgment kept him from speaking. He disapproved of fat and made no bones about telling Mother so. He and Mother were of one mind about diet. It was the fat that had gotten to my father, they believed, not art or madness at all. They were determined to save me from the same fate.

Mother stood up from the table and cleared her throat. Her skin was reddened by the glow of the sun, her chignon brighter than I'd ever seen it before. Florida was agreeing with her, I had to admit. In all the years my father was alive, I couldn't remember ever having seen her with a sunburn.

"Stan and I would like you to come down to the alley with us," Mother said. She glanced over at the Kingpin. He blinked at her, a secret signal. "That is, if you feel up to it."

His teeth were coated with milk and bits of granola. What was it about him that made Mother so happy? I wondered. His eyes were narrow and without a hint of brightness; he had none of my father's vigor. Was it the way he called her name, his scream of passion at the moment of release? Or did she secretly dream of herself pinned between Earl Anthony and Dick Weber and settled for the Kingpin as a surrogate lover?

I swallowed the last bits of my omelet and smiled at Mother. I thought of the bowling balls spinning in the alley, the feel of the cold floor on my face. Maybe the crashing in my head wouldn't start up again if I were brave enough to face the alley. There was something about bowling that Mother loved, though the sight of balls filled me with nausea. Yet I yearned for the smooth white hands that had touched me that night, the smell of flour all over them. The way the voice had spoken to me as if in a dream. If it meant seeing those hands again, I was willing to give it another try.

"Sure," I said, feeling at the ribbon in my hair. "I've got nothing better to do."

Mother and the Kingpin beamed at me, their teeth glistening under the light. To have me in on their bowling was more than they both had hoped for, I could see it in their eyes.

THE KINGPIN got us the premiere lane. Number 36, he said, had the best shine, the most desirable oiling for the spinning of a ball. You almost had to fight to avoid a strike. When he opened this bowling alley, he'd hired engineers to adhere to all of the American Bowling Congress' regulations, calculating the precise amount of oil to apply for optimal revolutions—or "revs," as the Kingpin called them. Bowling had changed a great deal since Dick Weber's day. Like anything else, it had a history. In Weber's time you had nothing to go on but a sixteen pound rubber ball and skill to see you through. They'd gone from hard rubber to plastic before settling in on the right material. Now there was so much to consider—proper urethane treatment and balls made of resin, oil slicked lanes and a frightening hook. Technology had made it a whole new game.

"People tend to think that bowling is not very involved," he said, leaning forward to whisper in my ear. "But there's a lot more to bowling than meets the eye."

He shoved his hands in his pockets, the outline of his thumbs pulsing under his corduroy pants. I kept my eyes averted, stared at the racks of bowling balls and held my breath.

We settled into the plastic chairs with Bessie at the helm keeping score. I wanted to be a spectator, but Mother insisted that I take my place in the lineup. The Kingpin brought me a pair of size nine shoes and a black ball with a gold star. I sat next to Bessie at the table and nudged her elbow. She nodded at me and squeezed my hand. We were both remembering that fateful night at the bowling alley when I'd first laid eyes on the Kingpin. If anyone had told me that night that two months later I'd be sitting in a bowling alley in Florida with the Kingpin as my stepfather, I never would have believed them.

When it was my turn Mother and the Kingpin clapped and whistled through their teeth. "Come on, Frances, you can do it," Mother called. I picked up the bowling ball and lined my feet up with the arrows. The ball was heavy, but I lifted it with both hands and sniffed. It smelled of sweaty palms and stale breath, the stench of nervous hope.

The Kingpin came up to me and showed me how to point my thumb, how to keep my eyes on the arrows and aim to the left of the ten pin, never head-on. He stood behind me and reached around to lay his hand over mine as I cupped the ball.

"Just let the oil help you along," he whispered, his hot breath in my ear. "I'll bet you have a fabulous hook."

As I shuffled up to the foul line, my shoes squeaked on the floor with my short, halting steps. At the last second I brought my arm back and released the ball, purposely aiming my thumb at the gutter. *There goes my future,* I thought, as the star went spinning, flashing on the face of the ball and then disappearing again.

I turned my back to the pins and heard the crash behind me.

"Strike!" the Kingpin screamed.

I looked up in disbelief as I saw the last of the pins carted away by the sliding machine. Mother jumped up and kissed me, her wet lips pressed to my face in a kiss that lingered even after she let go. The Kingpin grabbed my hand and pumped it up and down.

"She's a natural," he said, laying his hand over his chest with pride.

I shuffled back to my seat and watched as Bessie drew a large x in the box next to my name. We didn't look at each other. I sat for a long time examining my hands, the knobs of my knuckles, the cuticles chewed away in raw spots of flaking skin. After all the years of trying to shape clay, of struggling to create something which had not existed before, this was what I was reduced to. My only success— a strike.

WHEN THE GAME was over I went to buy myself a soda at the snack bar. Mother said the Kingpin would treat me to anything I wanted after my magnificent performance, but I didn't want what he had to give me. I sat on a stool and counted out some dollar bills. No matter what they said about fat and cholesterol, I was determined to have some pizza.

The man behind the counter had his back to me, but I could see the slow movement of his hands as he smoothed the pizza dough over and over again, his fingers sifting flour with a liquid grace. His hands were pale and fine-boned, sprinkling cheese, fingers fluttering like silent birds. I couldn't take my eyes off them, the way he pinched the dough so lovingly, fingers moving together and opening to let the cheese fly away. Under the sheer white apron, the bluish hint of underwear seams circled his hips. The flesh twitched between my legs.

When he turned to me I felt the breath catch in my throat. He leaned forward on the counter, fingers splayed across the white formica. They were squared at the edges, the half-moons of his nails a sharp white against a backdrop of pink. Across the spread of his knuckles was a smattering of wiry black hair. He looked up at me, a smirk playing at the corner of his lips.

"It's you," he said.

I had no idea what he meant. His eyes were round and dark and they looked at me with a fierceness like they knew me, had seen me before and knew just where to look. I swallowed hard and stared down at the floor.

"You're the girl who fainted," he said, and I felt myself laughing, my face flushed with color. I looked down at his pale hands, the sprinkled wiry hair.

"Yes," I said, "it's me."

He handed me a white paper cup. Without looking away from him to see what was in it, I drank it in one long swallow. The cool water moved down my throat, the ice stabbing my chest. I handed him the cup and he crushed it with his pale hand.

"I'm Dirk," he said, and wiped his hand on the front of his apron and held it out to me. His fingers were warm and soft. Bits of flour swirled in the softness of my palm.

"Frances," I said. He didn't let go. I had to fight the urge to lift his hand to my face and sniff it, to take the high yeast up my nose and down into my lungs.

Finally he took the hand away and opened one of the ovens, peering inside.

"I make pizza," he said in a low voice, "but that's not all I do."

It was as if someone had spoken to me in a secret language I'd been waiting all my life to hear. In the bits of conversation I could remember having with my father, he always spoke cryptically, as if unwilling to reveal any more of himself than he had to. Yet at the same time telling me everything.

Out of the corner of my eye I saw the Kingpin heading toward us, his wingtips shining, arms moving forward as if to tell the world about all the places he was headed. I wanted to reach over and grab Dirk by the apron, snuff flour up my nose. *Save me*, I wanted to say. *You don't know what the Kingpin wants.*

"What do you do?" Dirk said in this gravelly voice, just before the Kingpin was upon us.

I thought about the words I might use to describe myself. What exactly did I do, I wondered, that a stranger might understand? I preserved chainsaw men, struggled to sculpt sharks that came out deformed. I had a father who went crazy in the basement and now I lived with a bowler who wanted to take his place. But none of these things seemed right.

"I haven't found out yet," I said, and as soon as I said it, the truth of it hit me full force.

Suddenly the Kingpin draped his arm around my waist. His long cool fingers curved over my hip, drumming against my skin. Behind him Mother giggled to Bessie and poked at her chignon with her fingers. I caught Bessie's eye and stared hard at her. She raised her eyebrows and stood behind Mother, watching.

Dirk turned back to the pizza dough, his shoulders circling in time with the movement of his hands. The Kingpin pressed his hand into my hip and whispered that on a day like this one, pizza was fine by him. He barked orders for low-fat cheese and pepperoni, a thick cholesterol-free crust. I twisted in my seat to shake off his hand but it didn't move.

"We're a family of bowlers," the Kingpin shouted, his hand finally releasing my hip and coming up to pat me on the back. Mother took the stool next to mine and wrapped her manicured hands around my arm. Her tan against the whiteness of my own arm was striking. "Isn't that right, Frances?" the Kingpin asked.

All of their eyes were on me—the Kingpin with his narrow slits, Mother with her pale blue eye shadow and heavy mascara, and Bessie, wide-eyed, eyes framed in dark circles—they were all waiting for me to say it. Dirk kept his back to me but I could feel him waiting, too.

"I suppose so," was all I could manage.

As Dirk slid the pie ever-so-slowly into the oven, my face burned. They went on praising me about the wonderful strikes I'd bowled, how Bessie was learning to keep score like a pro, how bowling was all that any of us needed. When the pizza was ready they devoured it, scooping up slices and filling their mouths with the sweet sauce and melted cheese. My slice sat on the white paper plate, untouched. Dirk smiled at me, his teeth showing beneath his upper lip. I heard the bowling balls spinning in the distance, thought of the pins shooting out in all directions as I made strike after strike. After watching the painstaking shaping of the dough, the loving way he'd applied sauce like a thin coat of paint, I could not bring myself to eat it.

AT HOME Mother lay on the sofa with her knees up to her chest: a ball of pain. Since the Kingpin had mandated his no-fat diet, the shock of the pizza had wrought havoc upon her.

"I'm dying, I'm dying," she repeated like a mantra. Bessie pressed a blue washcloth to Mother's face and spoke to her in a whisper.

"It's all right, honey," Bessie said. "You've lived through worse than this."

The Kingpin paced the floors, fists clenched at his sides. I sat in a corner chair sipping ice water to quell the burning hunger in my stomach. Since I hadn't eaten the pizza, I didn't see how I could justify putting anything else into my mouth. I wanted to see how the Kingpin would handle himself in a crisis, now that the sheen of bowling balls and happiness had gone out of their lives in the clutches of indigestion. Mother moaned and called out to him to save her.

"Stan," she said, "it was that pizza man. He's gone and poisoned me."

Bessie got up from the sofa and the Kingpin took her place, wrapping his thick hands around Mother's. The chignon had come loose, the tangle of blonde hair jutting out from the sides of her head like a pair of wings. I pulled at Bessie's sleeve and whispered in her ear.

"The honeymoon's over," I said, and I couldn't stop myself from laughing.

After a few minutes of cooing to Mother, the Kingpin stood up and ran a hand through his slicked hair. Mother rocked back and forth on the sofa, her teeth clenched. I waited for her to call my name, to come and comfort her, rub my hands over her smooth belly the way I had when I was a little girl. But my name never came to her lips.

"From now on," the Kingpin said, raising his arm in the air and pointing an accusing finger at Bessie and me, "there will be nothing but salads. No more pizza for this family. The pizza man must go."

I felt myself double over, as if I'd been kicked in the stomach. The thought of those hands, so white and pale with flour, flew through my mind like a pair of wild birds. The outline of his briefs beckoned to me beneath the stark white apron. I wanted nothing more than to see them again. The Kingpin wanted to take them away, like so many things he'd taken from me.

"No," I said, as simple as that.

My voice came out louder than I'd expected it to. It reverberated against the walls, the wood paneling seeming to vibrate all around us. Bessie's hand flew over my mouth, but I pushed it away. Mother sat up and stared at me, her eyes wide, the hair shooting up in a blonde spray from the top of her head.

"What did you say?" Mother said. The color had drained from her face, blue veins thumping beneath her skin. She glanced over at the Kingpin and waited for him to say something but he pressed his lips tight against his teeth.

"I said 'no,'" I repeated and crossed my arms over my chest.

The blood thumped in my jaw, heat rising in my face. All three of them stared at me like they couldn't believe I'd had the gall to defy the Kingpin in the wake of Mother's suffering. If he'd no longer let us eat pizza, I thought, what would be next? Long nights of plain ice water and low-fat doughnuts shaped like bowling balls? The thought of never seeing those hands on the dough again was more depressing to me than anything.

Bessie leaned over and squeezed my hand. She looked into my eyes for a long time, her fingers wrapped around mine. Her eyes were clear and full of water.

"I've got to go with Frances on this," she said. "Eating salads is one thing, Stan, but getting rid of the pizza man is something else altogether. We all have to work for a living."

Bessie, the voice of authority. She knew just how to hit the Kingpin where he lived. Calling him Stan and appealing to his sense of right and wrong. The Kingpin knew nothing about art, there was no denying that, but he had the good sense to believe in the working man. I had to give him that.

Bessie and I held hands for a long time. Mother lay back on the sofa, pulled her knees up to her chest and sighed. She knew when she'd been defeated, and would never cross Bessie, no matter what was at stake. She patted the Kingpin's arm and closed her eyes.

"Maybe it was just the cheese that got to me, all the excitement," she said. "I haven't had anything like pizza in so long. I can't understand why Frances likes it so much."

The Kingpin nodded and tried to run his hand through her stiff blonde hair. His fingers got caught in a nest of hairspray, and pulled at the hair with both hands to try to dislodge his fingers. Mother gave a little whimper of pain. The fingers came loose all at once and he stared down at them, drumming them in his lap. I took a sip of the ice water and then spit it back into my glass.

LATER THAT NIGHT Bessie came into my room and sat on the bed. She picked up one of the chainsaw men from the shelf above my head and ran her finger over the smoothness of the long arms, down to the metal of the chainsaw. Over and over she stroked it, humming in her throat all the time. I tried to keep my eyes averted but couldn't stop myself from staring at the movement of her fingers, slow and deliberate over the chainsaw, one tooth at a time.

Finally she opened her eyes and cradled the figure in her lap. "So," she said. "Tell me about the man who makes pizza."

She lay down beside me on the bed with the chainsaw man resting on her chest. I told her about the way his hands moved over the dough, the feel of warm flour sifting through my fingers. The way he'd looked at me with eyes that kept on seeing.

"His name is Dirk," I said.

I nestled my head against Bessie's shoulder and listened

to the rhythms of her breath. It was like being a kid again, the softness of Bessie against me, and the chainsaw men all around us. We fell asleep that way, our shoulders touching. If art never came for me, if I were never able to transform myself with a vision the way my father had, at least I could still count on moments like this to see me through.

I WOKE UP early the next morning and took a shower before anyone else was awake. Bessie was snoring softly in my room, and I could hear Mother fighting off the last bits of her indigestion. I spent a long time under the water, the warm needles pulsing over my breasts and down the lengths of my legs. I imagined they were fingers pressing into me, molding my flesh, smoothing the rough spots of my skin and leaving me clean and new.

I got dressed and went to sit out on the deck for some early morning sun. The Kingpin was sitting at the picnic table among a trio of pastel bowling balls—flaming pink, aqua blue, and a deep orange that reflected the sun. He had his hands on them with his eyes closed, stroking them in long circling motions. The briefest of smiles lingered on his lips. I stood there watching him with the balls, his head tilted back in the morning sun.

For a minute I considered going back to my bedroom or moving into the living room to watch some early-morning talk shows. To let the Kingpin have his moment in peace. But I didn't want to wake the others. The fact that the Kingpin and I were both up at the same time intrigued me. I pulled open the door and walked over to sit next to him at the picnic table.

I sat beside him in one of the wooden chairs and waited. He continued to stroke the balls with his head back, keep-ing his eyes closed. I made a little coughing sound in my throat to let him know I was there. Even the Kingpin deserved some dignity.

He tilted his head toward me and nodded, still without opening his eyes.

"You like the pizza man," he said. His voice was flat and resigned.

The heat rushed to my face. How was it that the Kingpin knew so much about me?

"Dirk," I said, my voice just as flat.

He smiled, the points of his teeth moving down over his lips. "Yes, Dirk," he said, softer now. "You like him."

His hands continued to move over the bowling balls, making ever-widening circles. The sun warmed the back of my neck, my face flushed. I heard the faint stirring of Mother groggily moving to the bathroom inside. Mother seemed to take no notice of my connection with Dirk at the bowling alley, and yet Bessie had been on to it right away. Even the Kingpin had seen more than I'd ever given him credit for.

"Yes," I whispered.

What point was there in denying it? My emotional display the night before was evidence enough against me. I wondered if the Kingpin had seen the way I'd watched Dirk's hands sifting through flour and shaping the dough into a perfectly round circle. There wasn't much I could hide from the Kingpin.

"That's what I thought," he said.

After a few minutes I started to get up from the picnic table, but the Kingpin reached out and touched my shoulder. The heat of his skin shocked me. I froze as his fingers slid down and curved around the arc of my upper arm.

"Wait," he said. His eyes moved up the length of my arm.

I felt a squeezing in my stomach, a tightening of air.

Beads of sweat pooled between my legs. He let go of me and patted the seat beside him.

"Sit down," he said quietly. "There's something I've been meaning to show you."

Blood pulsed in my jaw, a pasty film came over my lips. I smiled weakly and sat down, careful to keep our arms from touching. He took both of my hands in his without looking at me and lay them on top of the flaming pink bowling ball. With his fingers lightly gripping my wrists, he moved my hands in counterclockwise circles, up and around and over the finger holes. I held my breath and squeezed my eyes shut as he eased my fingers over the surface of the ball. His fingers pressed into my wrists and kept the hands moving, the circles becoming slower and slower.

"How does it feel?" the Kingpin said. "What words would you use to describe it?"

My pulse beat heavily in my ears. I thought about how I might describe the sensation, but no words would come. The Kingpin laughed a little under his breath. I heard Bessie call my name from inside and jumped up from the table. The bowling ball landed on the deck with a bang that shook the sliding glass door. I slid the door open and closed it behind me. The sweat on my back froze in the air conditioning. I peeked out at him through the venetian blinds, but he already seemed to have forgotten me, his head thrown back as he ran his hands over the other two balls—aqua blue and a deep, deep orange that I kept seeing even after I snapped the blinds shut.

LATER THAT DAY I persuaded Bessie to take a drive with me down to the bowling alley. Mother was still nursing her sour stomach. The Kingpin fed her bowls of fat-free chicken soup at four-hour intervals, testing the temperature of the

soup on his wrist as if she were a newborn. After our incident out on the sun deck, I needed to get out of the house. I
asked if we could borrow the car, with the excuse that Bessie
and I would go to a local mall to buy cold cream and sani-
tary napkins. He said yes before I could finish the question.

"Go right ahead," he said without looking at me. "The
fresh air will do you good."

He glanced over at Bessie and then went back to rubbing
Mother's sour stomach. Mother propped herself up on her
elbows and croaked, "Don't forget the hairspray."

Bessie and I waved and were out the door. I closed the
door behind us and hugged Bessie as hard as I could. It was
like old times, Bessie and I alone on some secret mission
with Mother languishing on the couch. It seemed like
years since I'd had her all to myself.

"I know, sugar," Bessie said as she released me. There was
so much Bessie and I could say to each other without ever
using words.

Bessie insisted that I do the driving, that some time on
the open Florida highways would give me a renewed sense
of freedom. She strapped herself in the passenger seat and
flashed me a giant smile.

"Go to it, girl," she said, and we were off, speeding down
the driveway and up the road. I kept my eyes on the rearview
mirror, watched as the Kingpin's house grew smaller and
smaller until it became just a dark speck in the sunshine.

We played the radio loudly and sang old rock songs at
the top of our lungs. Bessie knew all the words. During the
commercials she told me jokes and we laughed at the
Kingpin and his wingtips, the way he was forcing Mother
to eat nothing but salads. I thought of telling her the way
he'd made me stroke the bowling balls, the careful way he'd
held my wrists as he'd moved my hands around and

around, but I didn't know how to begin. How could I explain that he'd wanted me to *stroke a bowling ball?* What had he *really* done?

I parked in the Kingpin's reserved spot marked with a big yellow "B" between the white lines. We wondered if the "B" meant simply "Boardman," or something more author-itative like "Boss" or "Bowler." Not that it mattered, of course. For a minute I wished I had a can of spray paint to cover the "B" with a "K," and laughed a little to myself at my private joke.

"'K' is for Kingpin," I said to Bessie, and she laughed deep in her chest, then motioned for me to be quiet lest any of the Kingpin's followers should be eavesdropping.

A group of people gathered to watch as we got out of the car and locked the doors. Bessie smiled at them and draped a protective arm around my shoulder. We were used to being celebrities. There was a time in my father's life when we couldn't go to the grocery store without being accosted by a swarm of fans who had been touched by the gritty realism of his chainsaw men. How ironic it was, I thought, that the Kingpin and his larger-than-life bowling alley had brought some of that excitement back into our lives.

We went straight to the snack bar and sat side by side on a pair of orange stools. My heart pumped with excitement. I leaned over the counter and sniffed for traces of flour and cheese, but there was only the lingering sharpness of oil and splintered wood. The counter was empty except for a yellow pad for taking orders and a basket of preheated french fries.

A man in his early fifties came out from behind the door leading to the kitchen and smiled at us. I glanced over at Bessie but she just smiled straight ahead and nodded at him.

I removed a napkin from the dispenser and tore it into shreds on my lap.

"How can I help you, ladies?" the man said.

Bessie kept smiling. "We'd like a pizza," she said, trying to disguise the laugh in her voice. "We hear the pizza here is the best around."

The man wiped the counter with a blue washcloth. His eyes were grim.

"There won't be any pizza today," he said. "We've had some complaints about the pizza."

Bessie and I looked at each other. The man wiped the counter in short circles. Bits of the napkin on my lap fell to the floor.

"Is that so?" Bessie said. She took a deep breath and held her chest out. "Frances here is the stepdaughter of Mr. Boardman himself and she finds the pizza to be the best around."

The man and I exchanged a brief glance. I kept my mouth closed, figured it was best to let Bessie do all the talking. The word "stepdaughter" hung in the air all around us.

The man swirled his washcloth around in a basin of water and sighed. "Yes, well," he said, "Mr. Boardman called in this morning to ask that Dirk be let go."

I felt a heaviness in the pit of my stomach. The Kingpin had betrayed me. After I'd admitted to him my feelings for Dirk and let him move my hands over his bowling ball, I'd felt we'd reached a higher ground. My cheeks burned as if I'd been slapped.

"Something about the cheese," the man mumbled under his breath. "Too much fat in the cheese."

I got up from my stool and ran through the bowling alley without looking back at Bessie, my hair flying behind me. Bessie's feet pounded in her effort to keep up with me. The bowling balls were everywhere, spinning down the lanes, the fluorescent green and bright turquoise balls coming for

me. I ran for the door and pushed it open, running straight
into the side of the Kingpin's car. I pounded the roof of the
car with both fists. Bessie grabbed me from behind, pulled
my arms to my sides.

"How could he do it?" I asked.

My breath was ragged, a surge of heat spread across my
forehead. Bessie lay her hands on my shoulders and tried to
calm me with her soft voice, but I could see nothing but
the sharp points of the Kingpin's teeth and the glare of a
bowling ball like a beacon in front of me.

We got in the car and I pressed the gas pedal to the floor,
spraying the crowd around us with gravel. "Slow down,
slow down," I heard Bessie say, but I accelerated instead,
spinning around the curb of the bowling alley and running
straight through a red light.

When we were almost home Bessie turned to me and lay
a hand on my arm. The air conditioner blew into my eyes,
the tears clouding my vision.

"It was Arlene," Bessie said in a whisper. "She pushed
him to do it."

Somehow I wasn't surprised. Mother must have seen the
way Dirk's hands had moved over the dough, shaping the
crust with his delicate fingers. She saw the way he looked
at me and sprinkled cheese like a pro. Pizza making was an
art like anything else, and Mother would know that better
than anyone. No wonder she'd had him done away with.

We went straight into the house without a word. Mother
was still on the sofa with her knees up, the Kingpin feeding her salad from a white porcelain bowl. I wouldn't even
look at her.

"Did you get the hairspray?" she said, more sweetly than
she should have.

I refused to answer. Instead I marched straight through

the living room and out to the deck that overlooked the beach. Mother's pink bowling ball lay on the picnic table with her name engraved in block letters, the one I'd had my hands all over just hours before. I headed straight for it and hoisted it over my head. With tears streaming down my face, I threw the bowling ball over the deck. Sand exploded as it hit the beach below, grains of sand shooting up toward the deck and then raining down below. I heard Mother scream my name, but I held my hands over my ears. A white wave rose up from the ocean and enveloped the ball. After a minute there was nothing but foam.

To VIOLATE a bowling ball, Mother told Bessie, was one of the gravest things a woman could do. And in the Kingpin's own house. She wouldn't even hear an apology. This was something she wasn't sure she could forgive. As if she knew the first thing about forgiveness.

"Ha," I said, loud enough for her to hear me.

IT WAS AMAZING how little I even noticed the change, how little I missed the sound of her voice. In the time since the Kingpin had come into our lives, we had less and less to say to each other. She wouldn't discuss my father or allow me to share my memories. To her it was as if he didn't exist. Now the silence was almost a comfort. At least I no longer had to pretend.

Bessie and I took our own meals together and left Mother and the Kingpin to their daily intake of salads. They ate salads with watercress, iceberg lettuce with water chestnuts, heads of romaine lettuce garnished with green peppers, and Waldorf salads with apples sliced like diamonds. For a change of pace they treated themselves to Boston lettuce with feta cheese sprinkled like bits of snow, snatches of endive and sprouts circling the bowl like wreaths. The only traces of Mother I saw were the bits of lettuce leaf she left stuck to her plate. I wiped these away with a sponge and rinsed them down the drain.

For the most part she and the Kingpin stayed out on the deck with the remaining two bowling balls. They sat side by side on chaise lounges gazing out at the beach below as if contemplating what had happened to the defiled bowling ball. Bessie said that Mother regretted the severity of her pressure on the Kingpin to do away with Dirk, but felt obliged to stick by her decision. She told these things to Bessie at night while I lay sprawled half-naked on my bed. I heard them whispering in the hallway, their voices low and urgent.

"She doesn't know what pizza can do," Mother said. "I won't have my daughter eating pizza if I can help it."

After a week of silence Bessie said that I should acknowledge the Kingpin even in some small way. Giving Mother the silent treatment was one thing, she said, but it was the Kingpin's house after all and for that alone he deserved some measure of respect.

"I see the regret in his eyes," Bessie said. "He wants you to like him."

At this I gave a snort. I wanted to tell her about that day on the sun deck, but what was there really to tell? Every time I tried to remember the incident, it seemed to disappear in a blur. "Then why did he go and do it?" I asked, hoping she'd guess what I meant.

Bessie shrugged. He was under Arlene's spell, she said. That was all she could come up with. So I managed to nod to him if we passed each other in the hallway or were caught face to face outside the bathroom door.

Day and night I dreamed of Dirk's hands. I moved

through life in a kind of fog, wandering through the Kingpin's house, stroking my father's men until all hours of the night, dragging myself from one meal to the next while always on the lookout for Mother. The hands moved in front of me even through my waking life, which in itself seemed a kind of dream. While I watched Bessie scour the tub or sat in the living room waiting for the next meal, the hands moved in front of my face. I could almost feel them on me, and had to turn around constantly to see if someone had snuck up behind me when I wasn't looking.

ONE NIGHT I dreamed that the hands appeared at the foot of my bed and stroked my feet. They moved over me with their soft fingers, sprinkling my toes with flour. Over my arch and down around the heel they molded me, twisting my feet into different shapes and elongating the toes.

Mother tapped at my bedroom door. I pulled at the blankets but my feet were buried underneath them, caught in a tangle of sheets. I couldn't bear to open my eyes.

"Frances," Mother said in a plaintive voice, "a man who makes pizza will be nothing but trouble. Before you know it your whole life will be covered with dough."

I thought of all the nights I'd lain in bed waiting for my father to appear in front of the venetian blinds. The frantic sounds of him snipping at the metal of the chainsaw, the heat from a fiery glaze. How he disappeared down in the basement, briefs and all.

I'd given up clay, agreed to keep my father's figures locked away in my bedroom like ghosts. I'd even gone bowling to try to please her. Why couldn't she see that I still missed the clay, that my father appeared to me every night in his underwear begging for water? The dough, those hands, had brought it all back to me.

I opened the door and crouched down on my haunches beside her in the hallway. We didn't look at each other, stared straight ahead, our backs stiff against the wall. After a time she leaned her head on my shoulder, her hairspray pricking my bare arms. I wrapped my arms around her neck and held her that way, rocking back and forth on my heels, Mother leaning forward to sway in time with me. The hairspray pricked at my skin, but I forced myself to keep holding her, not to pull away no matter how desperately I felt the urge to scratch.

CHAPTER SIX

*"Body of clay," the walrus says. I stick out my tongue:
"Amen."*

AFTER HIS DISPLAY ON THE SUN DECK THE
Kingpin kept his distance. We said hello on the
stairs and I ate the salads he made covered with
low-fat dressing, but never once did we mention bowling
or the incident on the sun deck. Certain things, we both
seemed to agree, were better left unsaid. Their sex at night
was quiet. When Mother whimpered, the Kingpin
shushed her in a stern voice. I didn't know if this was out of
respect for their privacy or because he knew I could hear
them, but at night all that came from their bedroom was
the soft splash of the waterbed and an occasional groan.

Mother had convinced the Kingpin to try rehiring Dirk
on my behalf, but nothing the Kingpin did would lure Dirk
back to the bowling alley. He called Dirk from pay phones,
even had him paged at a drive-in movie. I'd never seen the
Kingpin so urgent. For a week not even a splash of pleasure
came from Mother's bedroom. My sorrow, Bessie said, had
left the Kingpin limp with regret.

99

"We've got to show him you're all right," she said while I watched her scour out the tub one cool evening. "He's tried to get Dirk back for you. Can't you see the man's in pain?"

It was the first time Bessie had ever spoken so sharply to me. For the most part she remained on an even keel, no matter how desperate or headstrong I became. But something in the Kingpin had finally struck a chord in her. She lay down her scouring powder and wiped tears from her eyes.

"Let's go to the aquarium, just you and me," she said, laying a hand on my arm. "It will be like old times."

I nodded and drew a big circle in the white dust of the scouring powder. All of the excitement of the marriage, my resentment of the Kingpin, and moving to Florida had left me feeling more and more estranged from Bessie. How I longed to press my face against the cool glass of the shark tank, feel a dolphin's heavy splash over my face and arms. The aquarium was where we'd found Bessie to begin with. Maybe going there would help me feel like myself again.

"Bessie," I said in a low voice, "I don't know who to be anymore."

She ran her sponge under the hot water, scrubbed at a dark yellow stain on the side of the tub until it sparkled with whiteness.

"None of us do, honey," she said, but still this was not a comfort to me.

EARLY THE NEXT MORNING we composed a note to Mother and the Kingpin and left before they were awake. It was best to move out before their breakfast, Bessie said, before they'd have a chance to ask questions. Mother knew the significance of aquariums in our past and would have wanted to come along. After all, it was at the aquarium where we'd first seen Bessie, where they'd made their first

connection in front of the shark exhibit. How could we tell
her she wasn't welcome in what had been part of our history together? Yet I couldn't bear the thought of her hairspray in the closeness of the car, her chignon blocking my
view of the road. Besides, I didn't want the image of a
freshly awakened Kingpin to cloud my mind. I'd always
depended on the aquarium for clarity.

Dear Mother and Stan,

*Bessie and I have gone on a day trip. Not to worry, we
won't be eating pizza or browsing through museums.
But we won't be going bowling, either.*

*Call it sight-seeing if you must call it anything. We
will call it our return to the past. Be back before midnight.*

Yours,
Frances

I even toyed with the idea of adding a few xs or os for pos-
terity, but Bessie said it was unnecessary to take things so
far. We were off on a trip to find our way home again, she
said, as she pulled the car out of the Kingpin's driveway,
and what better way than to return to an aquarium—the
place where it had all begun for us.

"I can just see those sharks now," she said, opening her
mouth to breathe in the fresh air.

I pulled my seatbelt on tight and closed my eyes, feeling
the wind from the open window rush over my face. It had
been so long now since I'd dreamed of the emotionless eyes
of a shark, the jagged teeth and smooth gray fins. Longer
still since I'd felt the need for spongy terra cotta under my
fingernails as I fought to shape a perfect shark's head.

Bessie turned the radio up loud and tapped her fingers on the steering wheel to the beat. I smiled at her and tried to play along, but as we moved farther down the highway, the image of my father's face seemed to get larger and larger, while his features blurred. If we kept driving, I thought, before I knew it he'd smother us right there in the car.

We parked near the entrance to Seascape and locked the car door. More than an aquarium, Seascape boasted the largest collection of fish and sea mammals in the country. What better place to commune with the sharks? It was so early that the place was nearly deserted. The sun blazed down on us, the heat forming a sheen of sweat over my upper lip and under my arms. Bessie gathered up her straw hat and sunglasses and I tucked my wallet into the waistband of my shorts, the way my father used to when I was a little girl and we went swimming at the pier, when I would hold on to the waist band of his bathing suit and he would tug me along in the waves, the white crack of his buttocks peeking out at me if I pulled too hard. The smoothness of his back as I gripped it with both hands.

Bessie tapped me on the shoulder and pointed the way to the ticket counter. Every time I turned around I half-expected to see the Kingpin behind me, wielding a bowling ball and laughing. I had the oddest sensation of being followed.

"Do you ever get the feeling that you are being watched," I asked Bessie as she paid for our tickets, "like someone was filming everything you did?"

She counted out her change and smiled at me, her brown lips moist over white teeth.

"It's just the excitement," she said, squeezing my arm, "makes you feel like a voyeur."

We stopped in front of a large map at the entrance of the aquarium to figure out what we should see first. We couldn't look at each other. The memories of the day we first met were too strong, her shiny eyes and my hair slicked with dolphin spray from watching the show from the front row. I felt a lump catch in my throat as I tried to find the path leading to the shark tanks. No matter how hard I swallowed, the lump remained. The memories were thick in my throat.

"They don't have any sharks," I said, my voice sharp and strained. There were whales and manta rays according to the map, but no sharks. I stifled the urge to cry.

"It's all right," Bessie said, pulling at my arm. "We'll find something else to see."

I followed behind her, past the penguins in their artificial ice glades and electric eels sealed behind dark glass. The sweat ran into my eyes and down my chin, gathered in pools between my breasts. I found myself walking more and more slowly as Bessie hurried along the path. Let her go, I thought, watching my feet move but not feeling the slap of my sneakers on the pavement. Bessie's figure grew smaller and smaller in front of me until I could no longer see the tilt of her straw hat or brown arms swaying with determination. My shoulders felt heavy as I dragged myself in the other direction, away from Bessie and toward the opposite end of the aquarium.

After awhile I stopped at an ice cream stand and bought myself a cherry ice. I ate it with the wooden spoon, red sugar drooling over my lips. A crowd had gathered in front of a mountainous exhibit, swarms of people huddled together. Above their heads was a cavern of ice that cascaded down the stone walls, brilliant blues and greens shimmering in the sunlight. I walked toward them, letting the cherry ice run down the back of my throat, so sweet that it burned my tongue. The people were standing shoulder to shoulder, murmuring to each other. Bellows echoed over the crowd, a sheen of icy mist hanging in the air. I dropped the ice at my feet, red liquid splashing over the whiteness of my sneakers, and tried to shove my way inside.

"I've never seen anything like it," a man said, his voice hoarse with longing.

I plodded my way through the crowd, bumping shoulders and feeling the stabs of elbows at my hips and belly. As I got closer the moaning grew louder, low plaintive sounds like nothing I'd heard before. "What is it?" I said out loud. Some of the women were huddled together with their fingers plugging their ears.

When I got to the front of the crowd I felt myself swoon. Sweat poured down my breasts and into a pool between my legs. I felt my panties climb up the crack of my bottom, as if someone had grabbed them by the waistband and tried to lift me off the ground. My breath came fast, shallow and harsh in my throat. Black spots formed in my eyes, drawing lazy circles in the air like a dream. I gripped the cold iron railing with both hands to keep from falling.

A pair of walruses were mating on the icy moat above the water, their enormous bodies crushed together in a heaving mass of flesh. They gyrated together, the male on top, his tusks forming dents in the female's neck. He cried out, his tusks shaking as he roared with ecstasy. They pounded themselves together, flippers slapping against the snow-covered rocks, eyes closed against the sun. I gripped the railing with both hands, digging my fingers into the flesh of my palm. I felt myself opening, a light moving through me. It took all I had not to scream.

All at once the male walrus arched his back and flung himself harder and harder against the female. His snout quivered, the wrinkled skin glistening in the sun. I opened my mouth and held it there as the walrus roared. A man's tongue slid inside my mouth and moved along the soft inner flesh of my cheek. I kept my eyes closed and let the tongue devour me as the walrus screamed with release. Sweat soaked my panties in heavy pools.

When I opened my eyes I found Dirk staring down at me, his shoulders blocking my view. His eyes were black and full of laughter, his soft hands moving over my sides. I thought of the way Frank had kissed me that night on the lawn, but it was not like this, never like this. He reached up to stroke my face, and I craned my neck to see past him, but the walruses had slunk away and thrown themselves into the murky water.

"I've been looking for you," he said, and then he kissed me again, softer this time. His doughy hands let go of my waist.

My breathing was ragged, the air tore at my throat. I wanted to push him away and yet I reached for him at the same time. My knees buckled, but I forced myself to keep standing. It was like watching myself in a film, although I had no control over the action and it was not my head inside the camera. I wanted the picture to change, to move on to the next scene, but the walruses would not disappear, even when I covered my eyes with my hands.

Before I had a chance to answer him he was gone, his body receding into the throngs of people. I kneeled down at the railing and bowed my head. If I closed my eyes I could still see the walrus's head thrown back, the male's tusks resting heavily in the fleshy mate's neck. When I looked up I saw my reflection in the depths of a walrus's milky eye.

Some time later Bessie found me there with my forehead pressed against the railing. She lifted me with her hands under my arms and helped me out to the parking lot. I allowed her to drag me along, but it was as if part of me had stayed behind, sliding along the rocks with the walruses. She settled me into the passenger seat and fastened my belt. I turned to her and opened my mouth to scream, but no sound would come.

"Walruses," I whispered. It was all I could say.

She just nodded and hummed a dark lullaby under her breath. It was as if she knew. I closed my eyes and laid my head against the leather seat. The word turned around and around in my mind. *Walrus, walrus, walrus,* it said. The voice of a dream, but clearer than anything I'd ever heard before.

MOTHER MET us at the door in her bathrobe, her chignon a mass of tangled curls. "Where have you two been?" she shrieked, reaching for me with both hands. I smiled at her, even laughed a little as Bessie helped me over the threshold and deposited me on the Kingpin's couch. I was giddy with terror. My mind had opened up and could see in all directions. I mouthed the word "walrus" over and over, my lips and tongue moving of their own accord.

They hovered over me in a blur. The Kingpin came running in cradling a bowling ball in his arms. Mother's bathrobe came undone at the waist, and Bessie's hair kinked up her neck. I saw them through a cloud, their bodies enveloped by thick fog. My tongue grew pasty and thick in my mouth. As I tried to speak I imagined concentric rings spinning over their faces and moving down around their necks. The rings got smaller and smaller, spinning closer to their throats. If I didn't say something they would choke, I thought, but when I opened my mouth to scream, all that came out was a puff of air.

"I lost her at Seascape," I heard Bessie say, and then she and Mother were lifting me, Bessie's hands under my arms and Mother at my feet. I smelled clay, thick like feces, and the pungent odor of walrus love. Their feet shuffled on the floor as they dragged me through the living room. When I looked up I saw Earl Anthony and Dick Weber staring down at me from their glossy portraits, their eyes following me across the room.

Cold water splashed on my face. Mother held a bucket in the air and poured it over me, trying to bring me out of the shock. I couldn't stop crying, even through all that water.

"I've seen the walruses," I told them. Even as I said it, I could feel myself drifting, as if my body had split from my mind and was slowly floating away. Maybe this was what art was like, I thought vaguely, my mind swimming in the water. There was nothing I could do to stop it.

Bessie wiped my face with a washcloth, smoothed my hair back with her cool hand. I looked up at Mother's face, at the lines around her eyes and wrinkles carved deep into her neck. Her hands were rough and calloused against my arms.

"At least it's not a chainsaw," I heard Bessie say, and then the choking sound of Mother's sobs as she threw another bucket over me, water drowning my eyes.

I SLEPT THICKLY with the chainsaw men all around me. Mother and Bessie kept a constant vigil at my door, bringing me glasses of water and vegetable soup. I was running a fever, they said. But it was not a virus that burned within me, it was the heat of the walruses writhing without relief, a constant sex act with no hope of ejaculation. The frantic slaps of rubber love. I couldn't close my eyes without seeing them, their heavy wrinkled heads tossing back and forth with pained ecstasy, long tusks pointed toward the floor. How stupid I'd been to think of sharks when there had been walruses waiting for me all this time.

Day and night I hid under blankets to block out the visions, but couldn't stop myself from peering over the edge to see if they were coming for me. Every time I opened my eyes I half-expected to see a walrus on the floor, slapping its heavy weight into the carpet. My body was hot and cold, sweat clouded my eyes and a shiver ran down my spine that I couldn't seem to shake off, no matter how many blankets Bessie brought me. She sat with me on the edge of my bed, patting my hand to soothe me. Even Bessie seemed not to know what to do.

Mother brought in a game of checkers and fresh pairs of panties. I kept myself hidden under the blanket as she passed them to me. The panties I wore were weighted down with the crust of my fluids. I held the fresh cotton to my face and breathed in the sweet smell of fabric softener.

"You have to change your underwear," Mother said. Her voice was muffled beneath the piles of blankets, but still I could smell the hairspray clear as day. She nudged me with her elbow, but I couldn't bring myself to move. Part of me knew it was the right thing to do, but the other part shook with fear at the thought of the walrus appearing while I was caught with my pants down.

I asked them to hold the ends of the blanket down so I could change under the covers. "Since when has she gotten so modest?" I heard Mother say, but Bessie didn't answer. Slowly I rolled to one side and lowered my pajama bottoms an inch at a time. I hooked my thumbs in the waistband of my panties and took a deep breath. With both hands I yanked them off as fast as I could, squirming under the blankets to pull the new pair over my hips. The old pair lay next to me in a ball near my face. They smelled sharp and sweet, a wet terra cotta dream.

"We shouldn't have gone to the aquarium," Bessie said. "I shouldn't have taken her there."

She reached under the blanket and gathered up my dirty panties. I wanted to grab her by the arm, but I couldn't bring myself to move. I wanted to tell her that it wasn't her fault, that sooner or later I'd have gone there myself, that there was nothing she or anyone else could have done to stop it. Everything seemed frighteningly clear now, though I didn't know why.

The Kingpin's heels clicked on the hardwood floor outside my bedroom door. He let out a long sigh, wet, through his nose. I lifted the blanket an inch, just high enough to allow myself a little hole of vision. Mother jumped up from the bed and ran to him. They stood at the doorway with their long arms around each other. The Kingpin shook his head.

"If only she'd bowl," Mother said, "she could put all this behind her." She pressed her cheek to his chest and sniffled back tears.

I let the blanket fall over my eye like a curtain. When I closed my eyes I saw my father wrapped in the long brown bag of death, the zipper open at his waist to reveal a patch of torn briefs on his dead gray skin. Didn't they see? I wanted to say. This was how it must have been for him down in the basement. No wonder he'd sealed himself away.

As HARD as I'd been trying to hold it in, the pressure in my bladder grew so intense there were tears in my eyes. I peeled the blankets off layer by layer and slid my legs over the side of the bed. The house was quiet. I tiptoed across the room and ran across the hall to the bathroom. The porcelain was cold against the back of my legs as the urine set forth a terrible stream. I nearly wept with relief.

When I was finished I rinsed my hands under the cold water and took a deep breath. I sniffed deeply, drawing the air into my lungs and holding it. At first I wasn't sure what it was, but then as I opened the door the smell was over-powering. Quietly I stepped into the kitchen and turned on the fluorescent lights. They blinked and then the light held on full blast. I shielded my eyes from the brightness and then let my hands fall away.

Hundreds of pizzas had invaded the kitchen. Sauce was splattered on the floors, the high smell of yeast hung in the air.

I ran down to Bessie's room and shook her awake. She pulled on her bathrobe, her eyes groggy with film.

"What is it, sugar?" she said, but I couldn't speak, just held on to her arm and pulled her into the kitchen.

They were on the kitchen table, on the countertops, even on top of the refrigerator. "Good Lord," Bessie said, and she walked around the room, clucking her tongue and clutching at her breast. We found pizzas in the refrigerator, in the cabinets under the sink, slices stuffed down inside the garbage disposal. I felt sick with desire.

"Who would have done something like this?" she said, but then she shook her head and looked into my eyes for a long time.

We laughed a little and she put her arm around my shoulder. Together we sat down at the kitchen table and began to eat slice after slice, the sauce dripping from our mouths, lips crusted over with flour. Our eyes were glazed. We ate and ate until we couldn't eat anymore, until I felt my stomach bulge out in front of me and a fever in my brain.

"Give me a piece of paper," I said, and Bessie handed me a yellow lined pad she used for writing grocery lists and

keeping a running tally of bowling scores. I lowered the
pen to the paper and started to write his name, swirling the
ink around the page with my eyes closed. Bessie gasped
and clapped a hand over her mouth. She let out a loud hic-
cup and grabbed my hand.

I had written the same word over and over down the
length of the page.

W
WALRUS
L
W A L R U S   wwwaaalllrrruuusss
U
WALRUS

I looked down at the page and felt my stomach tighten.
The words moved out of my pen as if they'd written themselves. I held the page up to the light and wiped sauce from
my lips. Without looking at her I scribbled more words
down the page, my wrist shaking as I tried to get them
down as fast as they came to me.

Pounding bodies of
forbidden love,
a heaving ball of clay,
clay balls
baked in the sun,
in the oven,
a brief smile
lingering
through whiskers
through whispers
the makings of
a life.

Bessie picked up the piece of paper and tried to help me up from the table, but I just sat there with the pen in my hand, a scream welling up in my throat. I opened my mouth to speak, but all that came out was a hiss of air. Walruses moaned in my head.

Bessie helped me down the hall and draped me in blankets on my bed, but I just kept staring up at her, her face filmy as a walrus's eye. For a long time I lay sweating under the blankets. I saw my father kneeling beside the bed in his briefs, his fingers dipped in a Dixie cup. The heat from the kiln downstairs was unbearable. I wanted nothing more than to throw off the blankets and let my body breathe, but the sweat just kept pouring over me in a never-ending glaze.

FOR DAYS I drifted from dream to dream, scribbling poems on yellow paper and pasting them to the white walls of my bedroom. Within hours I covered one wall from top to bottom, the corners of the paper coming together in a mass of Scotch tape. I paced the floors of my room with my arms folded, muttering under my breath. At first I was afraid, but when the walruses were gone I lived in anxious anticipation for their return. I pressed my face to the window and called out to them in my mind. At night I stripped and danced on the carpet, shaking my breasts and pounding my feet.

After some time—it was hard to say how much time had passed—I became vaguely aware of not having bathed, of Mother tapping at the door and crying. Even as I listened to her sobs there was nothing that could remove me from myself, from the feeling of being locked inside the confines of my head. Only the walruses could bring me out. Only the poems were safe. When the words stopped there were crazy pictures and darkness, a terrible ache in my chest.

"You have to come out," Mother said, but I just shook my head and lay naked on the carpet. I dreamed of them day and night, their flippers slapping against the rocks, their heaving flesh and long powerful tusks. With the yellow pad and paper close by I ate the leftover pizza and rocked myself to sleep. Was this what it had been like while my father waited for the chainsaw men to come for him? I had no one to ask.

When the walruses were gone, the poems came more slowly. I struggled over descriptions of their skin, the shape of their pale tusks. The deadness of my life came back to me in a rush. Only when the walruses came did I begin to feel alive.

WHEN IT SEEMED they were not coming back, at Bessie's insistence, I returned to family life. There seemed to be an unspoken agreement not to mention what had happened in the days since I'd been to Seascape. I told no one about the poems, and ate my breakfast silently while the Kingpin polished his wingtips out on the sun deck. Mother stole glances at me and pressed her hand to my forehead searching for fever. She lifted my hand to her face and sniffed for traces of clay.

"You need to go bowling," she said. "It's the only thing that will help." She pressed her lips to the top of my head and held them there.

I thought of putting up a fight, but it was as if something had been stolen from me that I couldn't seem to get back. And somehow I knew I never would.

"Okay, I'll go," I said, and forced myself to smile, tucked a pad of yellow paper in my back pocket for safe keeping. I changed my panties three times before finally having the courage to leave the house. In the car I heard the Kingpin laughing at me under his breath, his bowling ball throwing sunlight all over the car.

He winked at me from the driver's seat and insisted I sit up front. He and Mother were going on with their lives as if nothing unusual had happened. They seemed not to notice my separateness. I wondered if they could tell that I'd had walruses in my bedroom for a week and had eaten a pizza in the nude. That my body had been lit with a fire that only a bucket of water could put out. They still seemed to think of me as poor sweet Frances, hung up on the memory of a dead father and going nowhere fast. If only they'd known where I'd been.

Bessie closed the door behind me and got into the back seat with Mother. The bowling ball lay in the seat between the Kingpin and me, the armrest holding it in place. I tried not to look at him, at the points of his teeth and moist forehead, but stared down at his wingtips instead. I could hear Bessie and Mother whispering in the back seat about me, but I didn't even care what they were saying. *They think I'm crazy,* I thought. And maybe I was.

When we got there the Kingpin laid his cowboy hat on one of the plastic chairs and cradled a bowling ball in his arms. The man from the snack bar brought us a round of Cokes in sweaty paper cups. The Kingpin was all smiles, bad teeth and pulsing gums. Mother stayed close to me, holding her fingers to my pulse and checking my pupils for dilation. Only Bessie kept her distance, hunched over the score sheet not saying a word.

"Here's to Frances," the Kingpin said, raising his plastic cup in a toast, "and to the hope that bowling will cure what ails her."

"Here, here," Mother said.

We drank down the soda in long gulps. Bessie did not raise her glass.

When it was my turn I reached for a black ball with a gold star, but the Kingpin stopped me. He pressed a cool hand to my arm.

"What is it?" I asked, and he grinned at me, holding his aqua blue ball out to me like an offering.

"Here," he said, "use my ball."

My jaw dropped, and I turned frantically to Bessie, who had her head down as she wrote our names on the score sheet. Mother was nodding her head frantically, clapping her hands and smiling. She had on her lacy bra and was jumping up and down, her small breasts bouncing beneath her white blouse. Her eyes glowed.

"Go on, Frances," she said, nodding excitedly to me. "Go on and use his ball."

I knew how much it would mean to Mother to accept this offering from the Kingpin, but my stomach sank at the thought. Still, I thought, I should do it for her. I nodded quickly and let him place the ball in my hands. It was smooth and warm where his fingers had been. Slowly I slid my fingers in the holes and bent at the knees. The Kingpin pressed a hand into the small of my back. I took four care-ful steps up to the foul line and pointed my thumb toward the middle arrow. The ball flew from my fingers and spun straight for the pins in a wild blue blur. It hit the head pin head-on, leaving me the fatal seven-ten split.

"It's a sign," Mother said. She fastened her chignon in the back with a bobby pin and chewed at her cuticles.

I stood there with my hand in front of the air vents for a long time, waiting for the Kingpin's ball to return. This was a fateful moment, I felt it with every strand of my being. If the walruses showed themselves here, I thought, then I'd know that I still belonged to my father, that I still had a chance to be an artist. And if I made the seven-ten split, then maybe Mother and the Kingpin were right: I wasn't like him at all.

I held the ball with both hands and breathed deeply, the smell of resin drifting up my nose. Mother and the Kingpin were silent. All around me were the sounds of pins crashing, the clapping of hands at a strike. I moved slowly to the foul line and aimed my thumb toward the arrow at my far left. In the distance a walrus's eye opened, dark and moist with desire.

I released the ball and fell to my knees, held my hands over my eyes.

"Good God!" the Kingpin screamed, and when I peeked through my fingers, I saw the walrus's eye open wide, the seven pin flying through the air and sending the ten pin smashing into the metal drop behind it.

The Kingpin wrapped his arms around me and lifted me in the air. He pressed his face to mine and smacked his lips against my cheek.

"She did it! She did it!" he screamed.

He held me like that for a long time, his arms tight around my waist. I looked over his shoulder at Bessie. She shrugged, her lips drawn down as if to say that it was out of her hands, that there was nothing she could do to save me. I kept staring at her, pleading with my eyes as if trying to send her a telepathic message. I'd made the split despite all odds against me. Where did that leave me now?

When the Kingpin finally released me I ran for the bathroom, my legs pounding the concrete floor. The walruses raised their tusks in the air and charged at me full force, roaring and sweaty in their pursuit. I made it into the bathroom stall and stood there with my pen ready to scrawl a poem on the wall when I saw the message someone had written in block letters across the length of the stall door.

Bowling is forever, it said. *You wait and see.*

As fast as I could I unrolled the toilet paper, pulling streams of it and shoving it into the bowl with both hands. I kept pulling until the entire roll was unraveled. The tissue fanned up at me at first but then sank down into the water. I could hear the walruses at the door, calling my name in tortured yelps. To drown out their sounds I flushed the toilet, the wads of paper spinning down the bowl, surging the water up toward the rim and then over my feet. The grief poured out from me in a torrent, a thick ball of mucus caught up my nose. For a long time I stood there flushing over and over again, letting the water spill over my shoes and out the stall where it headed straight for my ballpoint pen.

CHAPTER SEVEN

Tusks and balls, tusks and balls.
All my life is tusks and balls.

MOTHER FOUND ME LOCKED IN THE BATHROOM stall with my pants down, reaching for a pen that was just out of reach. The soles of my bowling shoes were soaked through, wads of toilet paper stuck to the tile floor. "Oh, my God!" she said. I fumbled with the lock but couldn't get it open.

"Mother," I breathed, "I can't get out."

She rattled the door, the metal slab pounding in the slot, the two of us pushing and pulling from either side. A roll of toilet paper spun across the room. "Come on," she said, and reached for me, her hands extended under the door. I grabbed hold of her hands as she pulled me out from under the stall door, my legs moving in the puddles of sopping tissue. When I was out she let out a long sigh, as if she'd expelled every bit of air in her lungs. I buried my head in her lap.

For a long time I lay there with my legs soaking, Mother's perfumed breasts pressed against my face. It had been so long since I'd felt her close like this, her lacy bra stabbing at me through the sheerness of her blouse, that I closed my eyes and lost myself in it. Even her hairspray smelled good. I lifted my face to her neck and buried my wet nose in the wrinkles there.

"Frances," she said, "what am I going to do with you?"

I shook my head, my hair rubbing against her breasts. It occurred to me then that Mother had never known what to do with me: all the years I'd spent locked in my room dreaming up sharks, the times when I'd snuck trays of food down to the basement, gallons of ice cream and trays of exotic nuts for my father to gorge himself on in the darkness. Only when we got a glimpse of him one day reaching for an apple that had rolled out the half-open door—when we saw how enormous he'd become—only then did she stop me. She hadn't known what to do to keep me away from him. As if there ever had been a way.

She pressed my head closer to her and rocked me there on the floor. I imagined my father on the basement steps, laughing from the side of his mouth.

"Don't you know they're coming for you?" he said.

Outside we heard the Kingpin's wingtips shifting on the tile floor. He banged on the door, urgent, fists pounding. Bessie's voice came from behind him, high and shrill with nervousness.

"Got to get her home," she said. "We can't leave her here like this."

Slowly I got up from the floor and tried to dry myself with paper towels, but the water had soaked through my pants.

"I don't want them to see me," I whispered to Mother, hunching against her shoulder.

She stood in the mirror and wrapped her arm around me, squeezing my shoulder with one hand and straightening her chignon with the other. She gave me a sad smile, her teeth shining through glossy pink lipstick.

"Don't worry," she said, "I won't let them look."

I started to pull her arm to hold her back, to keep her there with me in the quiet bathroom where there were no pins crashing or walruses waiting for me at the end of a dark alley. Like a little girl I stood there in my soaking pants, waiting for Mother to guide me. Together we went out the door and into the bright lights of the bowling alley where I felt myself spinning, my arms turned to rubber at my sides, the strength all run out of me as if I'd spent my whole life carrying armfuls of bowling balls and had finally been allowed to let go.

I STAYED INDOORS as much as possible, scribbled on yellow pads and tried to avoid the beach below. Bessie said I should make the best of life in Florida, that I'd be better off soaking up the sun than wasting away with a pen in hand and nothing to write. I knew the words were there, though, just below the surface. It was difficult to make them come when I was surrounded by bowling balls and the memory of what the Kingpin called my "miracle split." If I could only find a way to force them out, I thought, then maybe I'd feel like me again.

I sat at the kitchen table and waited. If art was about suffering, I thought, then I was in the thick of it. Every few minutes a sob welled up in my throat, and I had to swallow large gulps of water to stifle it. I watched the others move through their lives—Mother twisting and retwisting her hair, Bessie out on the deck varnishing the picnic table, and the Kingpin with his eyes on me. Nothing they did could touch me. The walruses were swimming in my brain, clogging my mind with water, their bodies heaving. There was nothing to do but sit and wait for the next phrase to come, a way out of the thick fog that had become my life. It was as if my life had become a grainy film, Mother's face moving in and out of focus, Bessie's warm hands that I could no longer feel, like someone else had slipped inside my skin when I wasn't looking. I was me, but not me, full of sadness and longing, but for what I didn't know. When Bessie told me to move out onto the deck so I could feel the sun on my face, I simply saw no point in it. I wondered if this was what life had been like for my father, if there was nothing to sustain him but food and the hope of a momentarily clear mind.

THE FIRST PIZZA arrived late one night after my fifth trip to the bathroom. I was sitting at the table pouring myself another glass of water from the pitcher when the doorbell rang. My vagina had grown swollen and puffed with desire. The heat surged in my vulva and held there, but I refused to powder myself or soak the flesh in a warm tub. The hotter it burned, the more hope I had for the words to return.

The Kingpin padded into the kitchen in his stocking feet. He was wearing an electric-blue bathing suit, and his hair was damp. When he moved closer I smelled the salt all over him. I pushed my heels into the floor, dug my crotch deeper into the chair and bit my lip.

"Are you expecting someone?" he said. I took a long swallow of water and shook my head. What use was there in telling him that I was waiting for a herd of walruses to carry me away, to pound me with their rubber flesh and leave me for dead? That my most private part was raw with wanting and there was nothing I could do to stop it?

He turned on his heel and padded away from me, his feet slapping the cold tile. The bathing suit was sucked into the crack of his buttocks, the swell of his flesh poking in the front of his pants. With my hand between my legs I pressed the seam of my jeans even harder into my flesh. *Let them come for me now*, I thought, but all I heard was the opening and closing of the front door, the Kingpin cursing under his breath. When he came back in he was carrying a pizza box in front of him, his arms outstretched.

"This must be for you," he said. "Everyone else in this house knows better than to eat something like this."

I just nodded in response, watched as he walked away, the spandex suit still wedged in the crack of his buttocks. I imagined Mother waiting for him in the bedroom where she would run her fingernails in that crack until he begged for mercy. One by one I ate the slices, the cheese swirling on my tongue, sauce dripping from my open mouth.

EVERY FEW HOURS another anonymous pizza arrived. They came around the clock at three-hour intervals, like feedings. Each time the doorbell rang the Kingpin hurried to the door and came back to the kitchen with a white box in his hands, steam wafting from the flaps on either side.

"Don't you know what all this fat will do to you?" he said. "How can you just sit there and eat when you should be bowling?"

I didn't bother to answer him. By then I'd changed my underwear three or four times. Bessie helped me with the first couple of pies, but then she belched and went to bed nauseous. Mother stamped through the house in her sheer nightgown and cowboy boots, but she had the good sense to keep quiet. She tried to get Bessie to tell me to stop, but Bessie said that I'd eat until my hunger was sated, that there was no other way to help me through it.

"She's got a burning need," Bessie said, "but no amount of pizza can help her. She'll see that when she's ready."

And she was right. I ate and ate as if drugged, but the pizza never seemed to stop the heat in the pit of my stomach, the nervous twitch between my legs. I ate and ate but still my vagina burned, the choked sob stuck in the back of my throat. Maybe if I grew fat and sloppy the words would come, bring me out of the deep well I was stuck in. I wanted to become huge, to set my mind screaming, all of their bowling balls shot to hell. But the more I ate, the harder it became to come up to the surface. I found myself gasping for air.

WHEN MY FATHER was younger, before he'd ballooned up to nearly four hundred pounds and lived only in his underwear, I used to sit on the edge of the bathtub while he lay submerged in a layer of bubbles. I couldn't have been more than five at the time, perhaps even three or four, yet the smell of bath bubbles never failed to bring back the sweetness of that memory. Sometimes we would play a game, rubbing Ivory soap in our hands and making shapes with the creamy bubbles. With his fist he would squeeze out the long swirl of an ice cream cone or pat a layer of foam like a wig on the top of my head. We would laugh and laugh, splashing in the water while Mother stood in the doorway shaking her head at us.

"Come on, now, it's time for Daddy to get out," she'd say, and she would coax me out of the bathroom while he slipped out of the soapy water. While he dried himself Mother would shut the door behind me, and I could hear them laughing inside, the smack of their kisses, Mother's laugh low in her throat. Outside that door I would wait, soap caking in my hair, for Mother to let him go, for my father to emerge clean and new. It seemed like hours until the door would open and my sweet-smelling father would ruffle my bangs, his fingers pruned from staying in the water too long. Afterward I would try to duplicate the game in the bathroom sink with Mother's dish soap and the drain pulled to keep the water in, but it was never the same when I played by myself. I could never make the same curling shapes or laugh as hard as I did when I sat on the tub, the porcelain slippery between the warmth of my legs. It was never the same without him.

DIRK CAME to my window late one night after the others had gone to bed. I wasn't surprised to see him. It was late and the room was hot, the air conditioner having shut itself off and the humid Florida air soaking through the walls. I heard the tapping, softly at first, then more insistent. On my way out of bed I knocked over a Dixie cup, spilling the water on the carpet. It left a large ring that soaked my foot when I stepped in it. With the bed sheet wrapped around me I tiptoed to the window. The others were asleep, so I pressed a finger to my lips as I lifted the window to let him in.

"Did you like the pizzas?" he said, a smile playing at the corners of his lips.

"Yes," I said. "They were just what I needed."

I let the sheet fall away from me. He smelled of soap and dried yeast, his hair covered in globs of wet flour. I took one of his hands in mine and moved it over my face, smearing my forehead with the thick flour, breathing in the sweetness. With his fingers he parted my bangs, moved his hands lower to draw circles over my breasts, kneading.

He leaned over me and slid his tongue in my mouth. I took it all in, opening my mouth wide and letting my jaw hang slack. The dough covered my breasts in thick powder, and he groaned low in his throat, his chest rumbling as he

moved over me. It wasn't at all like that night with Frank,
all that nervous groping and starchy underpants, my
father's silhouette in the window. Dirk moved against me
with purpose. His body arched against mine, chest pressing
against my breasts. I felt my body swell with wanting, his
erection smooth against the side of my leg. When he
entered me I stifled a scream, the long penis jabbing at me,
pulling at me with its urgency.

Dirk thrusted into me faster and faster. Our bellies slapped
together, hips crushed, bone against bone. The groaning
grew louder, deeper, his penis poking at me, stabbing. I didn't
know whether to cry out or just lie there with my feet in the
air and let my body twist. The more he moved, the smaller I
felt, until the whole room receded and all I saw was his face,
huge in front of mine, a forehead creased with desire.

At the moment of release I opened my eyes and saw the
shadow of tusks on the wall. Dirk pumped against me as I
held on to him, a huge gray shape moving in the dark. At
first I thought it was a dream, coming at me with its slippery torso and wrinkled skin. But then I felt the hot flood
of Dirk's desire and screamed. Flippers pounded the carpet, shaking the room.

"Bessie!" I screamed, as I pushed Dirk off me and scram-
bled onto my bed. He just lay there panting, his back covered with flour. The walrus rocked back and forth in the
corner, lifting its tusks in the air and groaning. Is this what
death is like? I wondered, the tusks throwing shadows on
the walls. Dirk lifted his head and stared at me, and I
wrapped the blanket tighter around me, my heart pounding. I couldn't tell if he saw it too, or if this one was for me
alone, if it was just my vision.

Bessie came running with a baseball bat in her hands, the
bat poised over her shoulder, ready to strike. The walrus

stood its ground, whiskers twitching with defiance. Dirk jumped up on the bed when he saw Bessie coming, but she didn't stop. She headed straight for us with the bat in the air, her eyes bulging. I buried my head in the pillow to block out the screams. My whole body shook, Dirk's seed running down my thighs, a hot glob of liquid that hung down from the opening, as if it didn't want to let go. I shoved my hands between my legs and kept my eyes closed, my face buried in the pillow.

"Stay back!" Bessie screamed. "I won't let you do it!"

And then I heard the bat swinging, the whir of air. The seed kept pouring from between my legs, pulsing out in thick drips, running down to the crack of my knees. There were screams, deep groans of pain, an anguished cry like nothing I'd heard before. The groaning kept on and on, distended, until there was nothing but the smash of Bessie's bat splintering on the floor.

Bessie was crying, the broken end of the bat still clenched in her fists. I rolled over onto my side, the semen stuck to my inner thighs. Dirk's hands cupped his crotch. Flour smeared his face and chest, swirled down the length of his thighs. I tugged the bed sheet around my shoulders and sat there not knowing what to do next. How did one behave, I thought, when you'd been deflowered by a walrus? Bessie wiped her eyes and tossed the bat in the corner, her shoulders heaving. From the corner of my eye I saw Dirk shifting his weight from one foot to the other, hair poking out from beneath his cupped hands. His mouth was covered in sauce. The shadow of a pair of tusks hung on the closet door, my father's chainsaw men behind them in silhouette.

Dirk let his hands fall to his sides and stood there naked, his erection in the air, curved upward toward the ceiling. The shadows shifted on the wall.

"Now do you know what you do?" he said.

He picked up the broken baseball bat and handed it back to Bessie. She just nodded at him, her eyes swollen, her hands covered in long splinters. Without looking back at me he walked across to the open window, reached down for his apron, and swung one leg over the side. I felt myself floating, my feet going numb and my head full of air. The sheets were soaked between my legs, slick with our bloody lovemaking, a salty mess. He pressed a finger to his lips and pointed at the shadow, his white finger stabbing the air. I held my breath as he jumped down.

My whole body was covered with flour. It stuck in my hair, streaks of powder in my bangs, grains falling in my eyes. Bessie sat at the edge of my bed picking splinters from the palm of her hand, pinching with her fingernails and plucking them one by one. Inside my head my father did a wild dance, the rolls of flesh shaking as he gyrated, his head covered in soap. A bowling ball shifted in the corner of the room. Bessie laid a splintered hand on my shoulder and sighed.

"They're coming for me, Bessie," I said, and she just nodded, wiping the flour from my bangs with her fingertips.

I lay back in bed and stared up at the ceiling. The walrus twitched in the corner, shifting its weight on the carpet, the floor boards creaking. I reached for the pen I kept hidden under the mattress and scribbled my father's name on the pure white sheet. I rolled over on to my back and spread my arms out wide. A small blob of reddish semen squished between my legs and bled the ink in thick black swirls, smearing my father's name beneath me.

CHAPTER EIGHT

A walrus speaks in tongues. It lies, it cheats, it mounts you on the floor. Once inside your head, it never lets you go.

THE WALRUSES SLID OUT OF THE BEDROOM WHEN I wasn't looking and were screwing in the bathtub next door. Sometimes they flushed the toilet over and over until the singing in the pipes was deafening. They didn't care if I heard. In fact, I wondered if it was all a performance for my benefit, all this incessant humping. Nothing, I thought, not even a walrus, could keep at it for that long.

Outside my bedroom I heard Bessie whispering in a soft voice, the scrape of the Kingpin's heels on the floor. Mother's choking sobs. I couldn't understand how they had managed to go on with walruses in their bathroom. Every few minutes I expected them to throw open the door and hide with me under the bed, Mother's chignon pressed close to my cheek and Bessie on the other side, her cottony hair brushing my arm. Or for the Kingpin to charge through the bathroom door and beat them to a pulp with his bowling pin. Or maybe, I thought, Dirk would come in with a giant pizza and the walruses would gorge them-selves to death. But no one ever came.

They wanted me to come out, tried to get to me through Bessie. Notes appeared under the door scrawled in Bessie's handwriting, but I knew what they were up to.

Frances,

Why are you hiding? We know you have a boyfriend and that you want to eat pizza. We will not stand in your way. We know that you don't love bowling. Do you want to be your father? Will you never bathe again? If only you'd get into the tub. Think of how much better you'd feel.

Love,
Mother, Stan, & Bessie

I tore the note into shreds and threw the pieces up in the air. The walruses pounded harder, their tusks scraping the tile walls. I wrapped all the poems in a pair of my panties and shoved them under the door. On a scrap of yellow paper I wrote, *Do you think I've forgotten? My father died in the tub.*

I sat cross-legged on the bedroom floor and held my hands over my ears to block out the sounds. I wondered if this was how it had been for my father, all that genius locked inside an empty room. I wondered if the chainsaw men had lain in wait for him, if they'd chased him into his dreams. How terrified and weary he'd looked at night in my bedroom, with deep lines around his eyes, dark circles of sorrow. I wondered if he'd seen it in me then, the specter of a walrus hanging over my head, long curving tusks coming to pierce my soul.

THEY SAID my father weighed close to four hundred pounds when he died. I never saw the body myself, just a glimpse of his back while he lay on the bathroom floor, the thick arm that hung over the edge of the bathtub. When they rolled him out, the body bag looked huge, the top of the bag swelled as if he'd taken one last giant breath and had never let it out, like somehow death had inflated him. I stood in the living room as they took him away and handed Mother what was left of his famous briefs.

"I'm sure you must want these," the funeral man said, and he handed Mother the shreds all wrapped in a ball.

Mother just nodded. There were no tears in her eyes.

When they took him out the reporters snapped pictures from the front lawn. I was vaguely aware of Bessie's arm around me, the click of cameras, the surprise of a flash in my face.

"What was the cause of death?" someone shouted.

Mother took me by the arm and tried to pull me inside. Bessie pushed me through the door, tried to keep me from hearing the word.

"Dehydration," someone said. "All that fat but not enough water."

Inside the house I broke free from Bessie. I ran to the bathroom and stood over the tub, got down on my knees and let the clay footprints stain my jeans. I rubbed my hands over the floor and cried. When they came for me I shoved my head down into the water and held my breath, opened my mouth and sucked down as much water as I could manage. Bessie grabbed me by the arms to hold me back. I choked and choked. They couldn't stop me. Over and over again I plunged my head in the water until there were bubbles floating before my eyes and water in my ears. My back pressed into the bottom of the tub. The light was hazy above the surface of the water. At last the world was silent.

"To suggest that the work of Morton Fisk is eerily reminiscent of the warnings against violence in modern society is to disregard the male angst with which his work roars. Modern male sculpture has historically been replete with phallic images, underlining the threat of feminism in a patriarchal world. His Men With Chainsaws, *minuscule terra cotta figures emblazoned with metallic chainsaws in their arms, personify Freud's theory of the male fear of castration. The phallic shape of the chainsaws, whose metal teeth and protruding blade are the most prominent aspect of his work, are an undeniable cry for protection of the phallus. Clearly Fisk's work seeks to speak for the collective male unconscious in its cry for preservation of male dominance. Fisk's* Men With Chainsaws *are not a statement opposing violence (as many critics have suggested), but the very emblematic representations of the violent tendencies man has historically utilized in order to protect the essence of its own threatened masculinity."*

Have you ever seen a walrus smile
all these many years?
Why, yes, I've seen a walrus smile
but it was hidden by his tears.

I wrote the words across my yellow panties and pulled them over the top of my head with only the leg hole to see through. I sang this over and over again as I closed my eyes and danced around in a circle. The world seemed so much darker, I noticed, with elastic panties wrapped around my face.

The walruses pounded harder and harder, the water moving under the door and soaking my carpet, their tusks pounding through the walls. Bessie came tearing through the door with Mother behind her. They stood there in the doorway, their mouths hanging open.

"Bessie," I said, my voice hoarse from all the singing, "did you know that the birth of a walrus has never been witnessed by man?" I danced around with the panties on my head, jumping up to click my heels together in the air. "But what about a woman? What does it mean if a woman sees it?"

"That's right, sugar, you've seen it," she said, "afterbirth and all, I'll bet." She tried to stop me from dancing by holding me by the arms while Mother wrestled the panties off the top of my head. The Kingpin stood in the doorway with a bowling pin stuck between his legs. He reached down for the pin as if ready to strike me with it, shatter my head and send me spilling out all over the floor. *Do it,* I wanted to say. *You don't have the balls.*

"They're coming for me," I said, and then I fell down on the floor with my arms folded over my knees, rocking back and forth, waiting for the blow. If the Kingpin killed me, then nothing would stand between Mother and her love of bowling. And my father and I would be together again.

The Kingpin stood looking down at me, his lips twitching, the teeth coming down over his lips. Thick drool hung from them, his mouth widening to reveal a pulsing black tongue.

I screamed then and started to sob, my whole body shaking. They tried to reach for me, but I squirmed under the bed and fastened my hands to the springs. I hung on, breathed in clouds of dust, the springs digging into my fingers. My own mother had sold my soul to a walrus and she hadn't even had the decency to warn me in advance. I saw it all so clearly now. She knew they were coming for me and did nothing to stop it, just like she'd done nothing for my father. She'd let the walruses come right into the house when she should have chased them away with a baseball bat, like Bessie, my Bessie, the only one who knew. She could have stopped them if only she'd loved me more.

Bessie's face appeared from under the bedspread. Her cheek was pressed into the carpet, the light from the room coming from behind her as she reached for me with her hand.

"Come on, Frances," she said, "no one's going to hurt you now." Her arm reached under the bed, her dark face framed in the light. I snuffed a wad of dust up my nose and let go of the springs.

She pulled me out from under the bed, my shoulder scraping the metal frame. She wrapped me in a sheet and pulled me up into a sitting position, rocking me back and forth. The room was suddenly quiet. Mother's chignon cast a giant shadow on the wall. The Kingpin rolled a bowling ball across the floor at me. His teeth were covered in thick white bubbles.

"You're a walrus," I mouthed, trying not to laugh in his face. He just gave me this sad smile and draped his arm around Mother from behind, his cheek pressed into her chignon. Bits of drool from the side of his mouth lingered in the sheen of hairspray. Earl Anthony's features melded over his face, turned his brown hair a dirty blond, bowling pins jutting out from his ears.

"We've got to get her out of here," Bessie said. I wasn't listening as they mumbled under their breaths about what they planned to do with me. I lay down on the carpet with the bowling ball inches from my face. My father had lain dead on the bathroom floor with his legs spread wide, the chalky wetness of terra cotta between his legs. They hadn't let me near him, not even to feel the clay on his hands one last time. He was right, this was what happened when art was stifled by ordinary life. I had to get away before they came for me and took me too far, before I had the chance to find my own way in the world. If I didn't find a way to live with them they'd take everything, even my memories.

When i asked Bessie where we were going, she would only say that we were headed someplace safe. They packed the car in the middle of the night. The Kingpin dragged boxes out the front door. He had on long pants and a turtleneck despite the heat and turned away from me every time I looked in his direction. He knew I'd seen his true self. I wanted to tell him that of course I'd seen it, that he must have been crazy to think he could hide behind a pair of pro bowlers when there was a walrus raging inside him. But I just leaned against the car and laughed a little to myself, my breath coming in loud hiccuping snorts. The Kingpin edged away from the car like he was afraid.

Mother piled my panties in paper bags and made me promise to do what Bessie said. Bessie would know what to do. She'd had a daughter who drowned. I let her press her lips to my cheek but the walruses were getting closer every minute.

"I've got to go," I whispered, my teeth chattering in her ear. A stiff strand of her blonde hair caught between my teeth and I spat it at the ground. "Say good-bye to Dick and Earl."

Before Bessie and I got into the car I made her go back in for the baseball bat. The Kingpin went in instead and came out carrying the broken bat in one hand, the other hand shoved in his pocket, the thumb poking inside his jeans. He handed the bat to Bessie and she winked at him, like they were in on some secret mission. I wanted to tell her that he was a walrus, that it had all been a lie, but I knew that with Mother there she wouldn't listen.

Suddenly I saw the walruses in the distance, herds of them moving over the beach, a thousand tusks coming straight for us. A cloud of sand circled in their wake. Mother wrapped her arms around me, the hairspray bringing tears to my eyes, a wisp of lacquered hair stabbing my open mouth.

"It's never too late to start bowling," she said, her fingers digging into my shoulder. "You can stop it if you want to."

I pushed her away and slammed the car door. They were getting closer, didn't she see them, I screamed, and then Bessie finally turned the key in the ignition and pressed the gas pedal to the floor, leaving Mother and the Kingpin behind in a spray of gravel. I turned around in my seat to watch as we sped away from the house and down the street. Mother was waving at me, her arm coming high over her head and back down, the Kingpin with his arm around her waist. The walruses were gaining on them, their tusks pointing straight at Mother's back.

"Look out!" I screamed, but then we turned the corner and I couldn't see them anymore. I leaned back in my seat and closed my eyes.

"We made it," I said, and Bessie just nodded. She kept her eyes on the road, her face pointed straight ahead. The baseball bat lay on the seat between us, the splinters stuck out in the top where it had been broken off in a walrus's back. With my eyes closed I took a deep breath and let the air move through my open mouth.

I scribbled all night in the dark, letting my fingers guide the pen since I couldn't see the words. If the walruses got to me before we made it home, Bessie would find this sheet of paper and know it wasn't her fault for not saving me.

The world would know that after my father died, art was the only thing I lived for, and that after he was gone, even that couldn't save me.

We drove all night without stopping. Bessie said it was best to keep moving. She was nervous, I could see, by the twitching of the corners of her mouth when she spoke and the constant drumming of her fingers on the steering wheel. I leaned my head against the seat and stared out at the blackness of the open sky.

"Are we going home?" I asked.

I reached over to stroke the baseball bat that lay there between us on the leather seat. She just nodded and tapped her fingers on the steering wheel, stealing a glance at me from the corner of her eye. I smiled at her and squeezed her hand. Already I felt a sense of relief wash over me, a gentle pulse between the legs. The smell of my ripe body filled the car, sharp and sweet as clay. This was what my father was after, I thought, this kind of freedom. But at what cost? If art could transform me, then why couldn't I find a new way to live without the heat of walruses writhing behind my back and a bowling pin shoved between my legs? Why did I have to be so afraid?

I turned around in my seat to face the back of the car. There was nothing behind us but the reflection of our tail lights on the road and the darkness stretching out for miles. No holes in the road where a walrus might have been or the slick wetness of the sea. I reached inside a box for the chainsaw men and unwrapped them from the newspaper. One by one I lined them up across the back seat, their chainsaws pointing forward, shoulders touching.

"You see?" I said out loud to them, stroking the chainsaws with my fingertips. "We're going home."

I waited for Bessie to say something, but she just kept staring straight ahead, never taking her eyes off the road. It would be hours before the walruses would catch up with us, I thought, and days before we reached the safety of home. How long would it be? There was no way of knowing. But for now I trusted Bessie to get us there, knew that she would ward them off with the baseball bat if they came for me when I wasn't looking. She didn't even seem surprised by any of this, and in fact, acted as if she'd been waiting for it all along. There was little you could do to surprise Bessie. She'd spent half her life with sharks.

THE DAY AFTER my father's funeral I made a pact with God. At the time I wasn't even sure I believed in God, since Mother was an atheist and said that God had turned His back on us a long time ago, allowing my father to do the things he did in front of an impressionable daughter. I couldn't remember what he'd done that was so terrible, except for his penchant for consuming as many as twelve meals a day and refusing to wear a pair of pants, but Mother was convinced that these were not things for a daughter to see. And I saw no need for God in my father's life, since I believed he lived on a higher plane than all of us. But that day I told myself I believed, because I needed something to get me through the day. Bessie said that was what God was meant for anyway, a little help to see you through, nothing more. If you wanted more, she said, God was not going to give it to you; you had to earn it for yourself.

The funeral was a private service for family members only and a select group of art dealers that Mother believed would conduct themselves with some decorum. The photographers were camped out across the street from the cemetery and hovered around the edge of the gates when we filed back to the rows of limousines. One of them managed to get a shot of me walking with Bessie, my head down, a chainsaw man tucked under one arm. On the front page of *The New York Times* the next day was the picture of me looking down at the chainsaw man and the words *What a Genius Leaves Behind* in small black letters.

In the article the reporter had mourned the loss that the world would feel at my father's passing, and speculated that the life of a genius such as my father would undoubtedly leave a profound impression upon his loved ones, especially me. I hung the article on the inside of my closet door until Mother found it several months later and burned it in the kitchen sink with a host of other articles. I was no legacy, she said, and she'd see to that no matter what it took.

The next day I lay in bed with my black dress on and tried to work up the effort to cry, only the tears wouldn't come. I wouldn't take off the black dress no matter what, and Bessie had finally convinced Mother to let me wear it in peace. I even pulled my eyes open with my fingers, lifting the lids with my index fingers and pulling down with my thumbs until tears slipped out the corners. My eyes burned and the tears rolled down my face, but I knew they were forced. I didn't know why I couldn't cry for my father. The light came through the venetian blinds and made slats of light over my black dress. When I closed my eyes I could still see him standing there asking for a glass of water. And I'd failed him. He'd died of dehydration on his way to the bathtub. How could I ever forgive myself for that?

On that bed I promised God that I would drink a gallon of water a day, I'd never think of Frank or touch myself at night, if God would let me understand my father the way he'd always believed that I would. I said this prayer with my eyes closed and lay with my hands under my back to keep from feeling between my legs. And I'd never, I promised, ever look at another man in his underwear again.

But of course I'd broken that promise. By the end of the week I'd become so bloated from drinking water that I spent half the day in the bathroom. Mother thought I was in there trying to relive my father's death on the floor and forbade me to drink fluids after eight at night. And in a couple of weeks I was lying in my underwear again with my hand shoved inside, rubbing the soft flesh with the palm of my hand. Thinking of the night with Frank on the lawn, the curve of his hips against me, the promises. And then of course there was Dirk, who had shown me his underwear and a whole lot more, his stabbing penis up inside all the secret parts of me where I believed art lurked. Now art had come for me, but God had pulled something over on me, whether I believed in Him or not.

WE STOPPED at a motel some time before dawn. The sun was just beginning to light up the road in front of us, cast a soft haze over the car. I wasn't tired, but Bessie said she had to get some rest. With such a long trip ahead of us, she couldn't sleep in the car and expect to keep driving for days at a stretch.

"What if they come for me here?" I whispered, reaching over to hold Bessie's arm.

She closed her eyes for a minute and patted my hand.

"You need some rest," she said in a soft voice. "You need to dream."

I made Bessie go into the room first, check the bathroom and under the beds. She motioned to me from the door and I ran in past her, slamming it behind me.

"There are no walruses here," she said. She held up the baseball bat as a measure of added protection.

Bessie took a long time in the shower, her voice low under the shower spray. I still refused to bathe since I knew there could be walruses in the tub. Walruses could be anywhere. After all they'd left the ice for me and lived on a hot beach with nothing to cool them down. Florida was as far from home as a walrus could get. While I waited for her I huddled under the blankets and tried not to think of them, but every time I closed my eyes, I saw their enormous faces drawing closer, their tusks dripping with pizza sauce, thick globs of drool hanging down from their mouths. And then a white flash of my father's briefs with a tusk stabbing through the fly.

Bessie came out with a towel wrapped around her head like a turban. Right away she saw the look in my eyes and came to sit at the edge of my bed.

"Do you see them now?" she asked, passing her fingers through my bangs. I knew that my hair was filthy, the grease weighing it down, but Bessie didn't seem to care.

"Yes," I whispered, and she lay down next to me on the bed, her arm curved around my waist. For a while we lay that way, my breath on her arm, the coolness of the towel pressed to my cheek. After a time, I whispered, "If I drown like your daughter did, will you try to save me?"

She didn't say anything for a long time. Then she got up and brought me back a glass of water, lifted my fingers and softly plunged them in, the cool water swirling over my fingertips.

"I want to write," I said sleepily. Bessie stroked my forehead until the walrus's face receded, the baseball bat tucked under her arm, words and phrases whispering in my brain.

A wall
a saw
a wall saw
war saw
walrus with its head
cut off.
A tusk of
the husk of a father,
a brief
young girl crying
pizza sauce,
bowling balls crashing
through
a life.

I woke up in a sweat. Bessie was snoring in the other bed, her mouth open, her teeth shining between her heavy lips. Someone was banging at the door, heavy, insistent, the whole door shaking with the weight. Bessie sat up in bed and grabbed the blankets with both hands.

"They found me," I said. "I knew they would."

We jumped out of bed and huddled together. The door rattled on its hinges. My panties choked me around the waist, a pulse of fluid soaking my crotch.

"Is it them?" Bessie whispered, and I nodded, held her arm as she reached behind us for the baseball bat. We waited, holding our breath, the door shaking with the heavy punches from the other side. The words raced inside my brain, images of walruses screwing outside the door, tusks scraping the sidewalk, whiskers bleeding in cracks in the pavement. Someone would save us, I thought, a motel clerk on his early morning shift or a passerby on his way to work. Imagine their surprise, I thought, to see a walrus pounding at a door.

Bessie turned to me, the bat clenched between her fists.

"What should I do?" she asked, her eyes wide, her hair kinked up on the sides from where she'd slept on it, pillow lines etched on the sides of her face. She was trying to be strong for me, as she'd always been, but I could see she was scared, that she realized there was little she could do to save me. She'd had that same look the day she found my father on the bathroom floor when she opened the door and saw him lying there flat on his stomach, his arm reaching up over the side of the tub. I wondered how she must have felt when she slammed the door and found me standing there with an expectant smile on my face, only to have to tell me that everything I'd ever loved was dead.

I took a deep breath and let go of her arm. My panties were soaked with sweat, the hair plastered to my head. This was how I must have looked to her that first day at the aquarium, I thought. Only now I no longer had to go to the aquarium to see the sea life. The sea life had come for me.

"Let them in," I said.

I stepped in front of the door and spread my arms out at my sides. This was the way my father would have wanted it, a quiet surrender. If art wanted me that badly then I had no choice but to give myself up to it, to let my image take me over once and for all. That, my father would say, was what art was all about.

Bessie closed her eyes and gripped the doorknob with both hands. "This doesn't have to be," she said, but I just stood there with my arms out in front of me. She twisted the knob and pulled with both hands, swinging the door wide open, the knob smashing through the wall.

"Pizza delivery," came a booming voice.

Dirk stood in the doorway in a pair of torn briefs, pizza sauce smeared over his mouth and arms, yeast down the length of his thighs and over his chest. Bessie laughed and dropped the bat on the carpet. I ran to him, wrapped my arms around his neck and breathed in the flour, rubbing my face in the saltiness of his shoulder. He rubbed his wet nose against my neck, his erection stabbing at my hip. I tried to pull away from him, but he held me close and breathed in my ear, his tongue tickling my lobe.

"I told you I was a pizza maker," he whispered, "but that's not all that I am."

He pulled me closer, his erection coming through his open fly, rubbing against my thigh, moving his hips in a crazy dance. I tried to push him away but he held me there with his hands pinning my arms, his penis jabbing at my hips.

"Let me go," I said, but I couldn't move, his hips pressing into me in stabbing circles, the erection slipping between my thighs and back again, wet sauce oozing onto my shoulders.

Bessie came up from behind with the baseball bat poised above her head.

"Let her go," she said, her voice deep and full of meaning. "You just let her go."

He let go of me then and stepped back toward the door. His penis still stuck out from the opening in his fly. It curved upward, the pink flesh covered in matted white hair. He made no move to cover it, just kept standing there with it poking out at us, taunting. Bessie covered my eyes with her hand but I peered through the slats of light between her fingers.

"Get out!" Bessie screamed at him, her hand still covering my eyes, but Dirk just laughed and laughed, his head thrown back, the muscles in his throat pulsing, his erection throbbing in the open air.

I pulled Bessie's hand from my eyes. He moved toward the doorway, shoved a hand inside his fly. As he turned away he smiled, his teeth moving down over his lips.

"Have you ever seen a walrus smile?" he said.

He ran out the door into the sunlight. Bessie moved toward the door and gasped, her hand flying over her mouth. I didn't know whether to move or to stand there waiting for her to say something, but she just shook her head and held her breath, her eyes bulging. Slowly I inched my way over to the door and peeked over her shoulder. I screamed in her ear at the sight of them, a herd of walruses in the parking lot, lined up in front of the motel. Bessie wrapped her arms around me as we stood staring at them, at the giant cracks in the pavement, the rows of swaying tusks. A man in front of the motel waved at the crowds of people to stay back. Traffic was stopped in either direction, women and children huddled together at the side of the road.

"Yes, I have," I screamed out at Dirk, but before I could say anything else, Bessie grabbed me by the hand and pulled me out the door. We raced toward the car holding on to each other, the walruses pounding at the cement. They hurled their bodies upward from their rear flippers, hips swiveling across the cement. Bits of gravel stuck in the bottoms of my soles but I just kept running, feeling their heaving breath at my back, the tusks inches from my thighs.

"Don't stop!" the people screamed, and we didn't even after we made it into the car and felt the weight of a walrus bucking the back window, the whole car lurching forward. We sped out of the driveway and through the crowd. Above the walrus roars and Bessie's frantic breathing, I heard the people cheering for us, felt my heart surge with triumph as we sped down the highway away from the whistling crowd.

CHAPTER NINE

*When your father dies, as mine did, you want nothing
more than to play records in your underwear, drown yourself in a bathtub, seal yourself up in terra cotta bliss. But
it's best not to turn away. It's then that the walrus will
find you.*

WE DROVE FOR A LONG TIME WITHOUT speak-
ing. There was little to say after you'd seen a walrus. I'd known that for some time, but now I
could see the effect it had on Bessie as well. The hair on her
arms stood on end, her breathing ragged and shallow
through her mouth, wet puffs of sucking air. In the excitement we'd run out in our bedclothes—me in my T-shirt and
ratty panties rippled with stains and tears in the elastic,
Bessie in a satin slip that clung to her heaving breasts. I
thought of the way the crowd had cheered us, men and
women lined up along the streets as we ran through the
parking lot past a herd of walruses. It reminded me of the
times my father would reluctantly appear outside the house
to let photographers snap shots of him in his underpants.
Slowly he'd turn from side to side, his massive belly hanging
over the waistband, holding up his clay stained hands for the
crowd to see. He'd disappear into the house leaving behind a
screaming crowd who applauded every move he made.

People in other cars stared at us as they passed, slowing down to gawk at us through the passenger side window. We must have been a sight, the two of us half-naked with a gaping hole in the back of the car where a walrus tusk had pierced the metal. A man in a tan station wagon tooted his horn at us, motioned for me to roll down the window. I rolled it down, hung my bare arm out in the open wind.

"There's a hole in your car," the man called over the whir of the motor. "A hole the size of a fist."

I looked over at Bessie, her kinky hair still flattened to the sides of her head from sleep. We burst out laughing, slapping the seat between us. The broken baseball bat rolled off the seat and landed on my bare foot, hard, stabbing me with its splintery end.

I stopped laughing.

I turned to the man and stuck my head out the window to yell back to him. Even the wind couldn't force my unwashed hair to move.

"You mean," I called, feeling the wind moving in my open mouth, "a hole the size of a tusk."

He stared hard at me for a minute and then punched the accelerator, leaving us behind in a cloud of exhaust. I shrugged my shoulders and rolled up the window. The world was not ready for walrus stories.

For the first time since I'd seen the walruses at the aquarium, things began to seem clear. I thought about how Dirk had slipped his tongue so easily inside my mouth, twirling it around like it had been there before, as if he had somehow claimed me. He'd sent pizzas as warning signs, threatened me with his penis, shoved it inside to break me open once and for all. That was what I'd always wanted, to be broken, to have art crack through my world and send my soul soaring out of the deadness of my everyday life. In fact, since I'd been broken the walruses had never left me. But this wasn't what I'd expected, sweaty nightmares and pulsing thighs, a penis stabbing at me night and day. This wasn't the kind of art I'd hoped for. No wonder Mother had turned her life over to bowling. Nothing about art was easy.

"It was Dirk," I said aloud to Bessie. "Dirk is the one who brought them."

She didn't answer me, just nodded and kept both hands on the wheel. Every few seconds she checked her rearview mirror to see if there were walruses behind us, cracks in the pavement, a runny stream of fluid, the tell-tale signs of their desires. I thought about Dirk and his fine-boned hands and sparkling briefs, the smell of yeast under his arms, flour stuck under his fingernails. The way his hands moved over the dough, my body. I didn't know why I hadn't seen it from the start.

"I want to go home," I said, and as I said it I felt the lump in my throat rise, the familiar tightness in the chest. I nudged the baseball bat with my foot. It wouldn't be long before they came again, I thought, next time with Dirk leading the pack, his penis sticking out through his briefs, while I would struggle to ward them off with pen and paper, the only weapons I had left.

"Don't worry, sugar," Bessie said, "we're going to get you there safe."

Some time later we pulled to the side of the road and slept. We lay at opposite ends of the seat, our bare feet touching, the cool leather pressed against our faces. I remembered a time when I was a little girl before the chainsaw men came, when my father took us on long drives and Mother and I would nestle together in the front seat, my back turned toward my father and his thigh against me, Mother's face toward mine. It was before my father was famous, before the screams, before all the clay and dreams, the dancing in my bedroom late at night with the light splicing through the venetian blinds. I thought everything I ever wanted could be mine then with my parents on either side of me, the cool dry air of the air conditioner blowing over our faces. I was young and freshly bathed and my father smelled only of soap. Those were the pure things I remembered through the wall of walruses knocking in my brain, but even these things had started to recede. I could feel it now, that it wouldn't be long before even those memories were gone.

At midnight we stopped at an all-night convenience store for some snacks and coffee. The store was isolated at the edge of the highway, surrounded by a high grassy swamp on one side and an abandoned bowling alley on the other. You could tell it was a bowling alley by the color of the bricks and the dead neon sign in the shape of a pin. I immediately felt the sense of dread, the tightness in my jaw and between my legs.

"Maybe we should keep going," I said. "This is the kind of place a walrus would love."

But Bessie pulled in the driveway just the same, switched off the ignition, and pressed a weary hand to her flattened hair.

"We've got to stop some time," she said. "This place is as good as any."

Reluctantly I followed Bessie around the car to the trunk. The hole in the back seemed to have grown wider, the metal curving in on itself, leaving patches of rust all around the outside of the hole. In the trunk Bessie found some old bedsheets to tie around us. We couldn't very well go into a store looking like we did, she said. Even walruses could respect some sense of decorum.

I tied the sheet tightly around my chest, crushing my breasts under the flimsy T-shirt. Bessie draped hers over her head like a shroud, the sheet hanging over her bare arms. Together we walked into the convenience store as quietly as we could manage, but we knew there was no point in trying to be inconspicuous looking the way we did.

We gathered up our candies and water, a styrofoam cup filled with black coffee for Bessie and lined up our purchases on the counter. The man behind the counter was watching a black-and-white television and eating popcorn. He leaned forward on his stool toward the television to get a closer look. Bessie cleared her throat to get his attention, but he waved a hand at her and leaned closer to the TV.

"A herd of walruses stampeded through a motel parking lot yesterday in Pensacola, Florida," the reporter said. "Eyewitnesses claim that the walruses were seen chasing a young girl and a middle-aged black woman on their way out of the parking lot. There is no word yet on where the walruses came from, or how they might have migrated from their arctic homeland. Authorities believe they escaped from the new exhibit at Seascape some time before midnight. The walruses were recently acquired through a grant from the Nature Foundation as part of Seascape's recent addition of sea mammals. The young woman has been identified as Frances Fisk, daughter of renowned sculptor Morton Fisk, who created a stir in the art world several years ago with his *Men With Chainsaws*. Fisk was apparently found dead trying to take a bath. No one is sure why Ms. Fisk has been singled out by the escaped walruses, though her mother, Arlene Boardman, expressed concern for her daughter's safety."

The sheet fell way from my body as the camera turned to Mother and the Kingpin standing outside of the Kingpin's house. Behind them was a backdrop of a dead walrus sprawled on the lawn.

Mother held the microphone in her hand and took a deep breath. Her lacquered hair shifted in the heavy wind. The Kingpin looked straight into the camera, his lips twitching.

"I knew it would come to this," Mother said, her eyes red and swollen. "I tried to tell her, but she wouldn't listen. She wouldn't stop until they came for her, and now she'll have to run for her life."

The reporter took the microphone from Mother and pressed it to his lips.

"Do you mean to say that there is some connection between walruses and art?" he asked.

Mother raked her fingers through the stiff hairspray and tore the microphone from the reporter's hand.

"She wants to be just like him," she said, shaking her head. "I tried to get her to bowl, but all she wanted was to write, and now she's sorry, I'll bet. Now she wishes she'd forgotten all about him. There are some things you're better off not thinking about, and Morton is one of them."

The report cut to a photo of the four of us at the bowling alley, the Kingpin in his wingtips and Bessie in her satin dress, me braless in the denim skirt. We looked like any other family, I thought—except for me. My face was all twisted up in pain and I had this faraway look in my eyes, like I was there but not there, like I was trying to will myself out of my body. Then the picture changed again to a photo of my father on the front lawn among a crowd of reporters, one hand shoved inside the waistband of his briefs and the other holding a chainsaw man triumphantly over his head. I remembered that picture. It was taken right after his first show at the Guggenheim. His belly hung low, his chest smeared with terra cotta thumb prints.

"Fisk's work was the center of much debate among members of art's inner circle," the reporter said. "Many critics suggested that his art personified the workings of the tumultuous unconscious mind. Others viewed his *Men With Chainsaws* as a symbolic warning against a fascistic New World Order, while still others raged in debate as to whether his work implied the need for violence in a castrating world or sought to end the violence wrought by modern man in a rapidly disintegrating civilization."

The man behind the counter turned to us and shook his head.

"Sounds like a real nut," he said, laughing, poppy seeds flecked in his small pointy teeth.

I opened my mouth to defend my father but knew we should get out of there as soon as possible, that it wouldn't be long before the walruses found us or before the Kingpin came careening down the highway with a trunk full of bowling balls. But I couldn't move, just kept staring at my father's face, at the slot in his briefs where the camera cut him off, the look of desperation in his eyes. It had been so long since I'd seen him this way, fleshed out, without the color of memory or imagination. I couldn't believe how strange he really looked.

Bessie yanked at my arm, but I didn't move.

"Hey," the man said, stepping off his stool to edge closer to us, "it's you."

Bessie dropped a handful of bills on the counter and pulled me by the sleeve of my T-shirt, just as the camera cut to the Kingpin reaching for the microphone and pointing at the walrus carcass on his lawn. We hurried to the car.

Bessie slammed the door and started the engine. The air smelled of pizza.

"Did you see that?" I asked Bessie as we pulled out of the parking lot. The man from behind the counter waved his arms at us to come back, but Bessie kept right on going. "I'm famous now."

She nodded and rolled down the window, letting the air circle us in the small space of the car. I turned around to look at the man in the distance, craning my neck to see. The figure got smaller and smaller as Bessie sped up. I reached a hand in the back seat and realized the chainsaw men were gone. For the first time since we left the motel, I realized I'd left them behind.

I turned around in my seat and started to cry, heavy salty tears that rolled down my cheeks but made no sound. The tears came and came, but without real feeling behind them. Everything I was seemed to be trapped inside my head. I was vaguely aware of the tears, but it was like watching someone else cry, like the sadness wasn't mine. I didn't know whose it was. There were no words in my head but the image of a large gray body suspended in water. I didn't know if it was a walrus, my father, or a large melted bowling ball. Nothing of my life seemed to be mine anymore.

I didn't even react when we saw the roadblock ahead of us. Orange pylons lined the highway on both sides, a truck with big arrows pointing to the shoulder of the road. Bessie slammed on the brakes, and a man in an orange helmet got out of the truck and waved a flag in the air for her to stop. *Just keep going,* I wanted to say, but the words wouldn't come. All I could see was my father's face on the black-and-white television, the wavy lines distorting his features, his heavy lips opening and closing, rotted teeth showing through dull gray gums.

We stopped in front of the truck and Bessie got out to talk to the man. For a long time they stood there with the flashing orange lights reflected on their faces. The man pointed at me and then to the area behind the cones. I slumped down in my seat, the tears dripping off my face and down the front of my T-shirt.

The man tapped on my window with his orange flag.

"Are you Frances Fisk?" he asked.

I couldn't stop the tears. I tried to, but I couldn't stop. I nodded slowly and pointed down at my panties.

"I'm famous," I said. "I was on TV."

The man nodded and opened the car door. He reached for my arm and I didn't resist, letting him pull me up by the hand and lead me over to the barricade. I saw my father lying dead on the bathroom floor, my father in the bathtub, my father in front of the venetian blinds.

We stood behind the row of pylons. Bessie put her arm around me and held it there. I could barely see through the tears that just kept coming, though I couldn't feel them for the wetness over my face. The man pointed his flag at the deep crevice in the road beyond the orange lights.

"Walruses," he said, pointing. "It's the damnedest thing. All of a sudden they were all over the highway. We had no choice but to put them down."

I didn't say anything. The man walked away and Bessie and I stood there staring out at the dead bodies, their cracked gray skin, smashed tusks, bleeding snouts. Bessie held her arm around my shoulder and stared at me, waiting for me to say something, scream, laugh, get down on my knees. But I just cried, closed my eyes and thought of all the things Mother had ever told me—that it wasn't right for a daughter to see a father in his underwear, that art had ruined us, that all my dreams had been wrong. I heard all these things and yet I could still feel my father's clay fingertips moving through my bangs, the smoothness of a chainsaw man in my arms. The walruses might have been dead, but they had me just the same.

The man threw an orange poncho over my shoulders and led us back to the car.

"It's not something we wanted to do," he said. "I'm sure we'll have to answer for this. But we couldn't just let them take over the highway. People have places to go. We tried to chase them, but they just wouldn't go."

He gave me a sad smile and shook Bessie's hand.

"You understand, ma'am," he said. "The highway is just no place for a walrus."

Bessie smiled and touched his arm. As he walked away I saw underwear lines bulging from beneath his tight polyester pants.

I sat there in the car as they lifted the bodies away with cranes, teams of men shoveling away the remains all through the night. Bessie touched my hair with her fingertips, smoothing back my bangs, but there was no longer any comfort in that. They slid the walrus bodies into enormous brown bags and zipped them up, teams of men hurling flippers and fragments of ivory into dump trucks.

I wondered what would have happened if some housewife had been tooting along the highway and run smack into the side of a walrus. Or if a man with a beer belly and a pick-up truck had hit one head-on. Most people wouldn't know what to do if they saw a walrus in the middle of the road. Their lives could never have prepared them for such a shock.

Some time before daylight the photographers came and snapped photos of Bessie and me in the car. At first Bessie held my face to her breast to shield me from the flash, but

I struggled against her until she let me go. Then I opened the car door and walked out into the moonlit air, turning my face toward the cameras. One of the reporters broke through the crowd and thrust a microphone into my face.

"Frances," he shouted above the hum of the crane motors, the scrape of shovels on the pavement, "what would your father say if he could see you now?"

I took a deep breath and looked over at Bessie, who was weeping softly in the corner, chewing at her nails. I hooked my thumbs in the waistband of my panties and felt the heavy discharge between my legs, the grime over my skin from the weeks of not bathing, the strain of having a genius for a father. I turned to the reporter and gave him a sad smile.

"He wouldn't need to say anything," I said. "He'd take all of his chainsaw men and seal himself away."

THE NIGHT before my father died he visited me for the last time. It was late and Mother was snoring in her room at the other end of the hallway. We'd spent the day trying to break him out of the basement, and we were all exhausted, even Bessie, who usually was the last to fall asleep. I lay in bed listening for the sound of his weight bending the foundation, the heat of his kiln from the floor below. He was quiet that night. I wondered if the chainsaw men had finally come to get him, or if he'd finally drained himself of inspiration, if suddenly he'd climb the stairs in a pair of coveralls and ask what we were having for supper. Or if he'd gorged himself in one last frenzied feeding. There was no sound, only the creaking of the springs as I moved on my bed, adjusting my pillow and trying to stop the choking sensations that came at night when I was alone and there was no noise. Everything in the house felt exhausted, deadened.

He came when I was almost asleep, that time when the fog in my brain descended and the crazy pictures would start of stairways and briefs, a head full of bath bubbles and a wrinkled hand on my leg. I heard my door open and saw him standing by the bed, the briefs left hanging to his hips by a thick knot of elastic. At first I opened my eyes like slits, not sure if I should pretend to be asleep in case I would frighten him away. I lay flat on my back and kept my eyes half-closed as he inched his way toward the bed. The floor shook under his weight as he got closer, and I shifted in the bed, slid my hands under the sheets. "Dad," I whispered, "is it you?"

He edged closer to the bed and leaned forward. I felt his breath over my face, the hot smell of terra cotta sweat. Slowly he reached out his hand and moved it over my hair, his fingers dipping into my bangs and back out again. I closed my eyes and let him touch me, felt the clay melting in my hair as he smoothed it around in circles. I didn't know how long he stayed there, leaning down over my bed with his fingers in my hair. I must have fallen asleep, and when I woke up he was swaying back and forth in front of the venetian blinds, his briefs torn to shreds. As he left the room I closed my eyes, and it wasn't until that morning that I heard the water running and Mother screaming from the kitchen. The water seeped down the hallway and into my bedroom, soaking the carpet. When I jumped off the bed to run and see what had happened, I slipped on the floor, the water soaking my panties, dead wet clay stuck to my back.

CHAPTER TEN

I've watched my father die; I've danced with panties on my head. I've eaten pizza and made clay bowling balls in the nude. Best of all I've heard what a walrus says: goo-goo-a-joob.

BECAME FAMOUS. THE PHOTO OF ME IN MY T-SHIRT and panties appeared on the cover of every major newspaper, on nightly news programs and tabloid magazines. And finally, on the front page of *Art in America*. Beneath the photo were the words: *Frances Fisk: Legacy of a Genius*. Inside the magazine was a full color spread of the dead walruses on the highway with Bessie and me watching as they were carted away. In the background of one of the photos, a tiny spot you'd miss if you didn't look carefully enough, was a freshly baked pizza, the steam rising off the crust. I wondered if Dirk would find me now or if he'd go back to his life in bowling alleys, making pizza with his flour-stained hands. If he knew the walruses were dead.

Even after the attack at the motel, in a strange way, I missed him.

Mother and the Kingpin were waiting for us outside when we arrived at my father's house. The reporters had come out in droves. I knew they'd be there, that the Kingpin would be dying to see his face plastered on the front of a newspaper, his teeth glaring out at him from a magazine spread. They were standing in the driveway shoulder to shoulder. Mother's hair hung loose, unsprayed, her heavy blonde curls shifting in the wind. The Kingpin held a bowling ball up in the air in salute as Bessie and I pulled in front of the house. My cheeks hurt from the effort it cost me to keep smiling.

Bessie reached over to unlock my door and I caught her arm and held it there. The cameras flashed in our faces, forming purple and orange spots in my eyes. I stepped out of the car and pressed a bare foot to the pavement, feeling the heat rise from the warm cement and move up the length of my leg. Bessie covered me with a torn sheet as we walked up to the front of the house. I saw Mother's hand waving above the crowd, but I couldn't drop the sheet to wave back. A reporter came running and thrust a microphone in my face. He smelled of lead pencils and stale cigarettes, his hand covered in tiny spots of black ink.

"Frances," he said, "tell us what it's like to be chased by a walrus."

He handed me the microphone and held a pencil to his yellow pad, waiting to scribble whatever I might say. It was such an odd sensation to have someone wait with bated breath for your next syllable, as if what you might have to say could change the world. Even Mother stopped short as she ran toward me, her hand raking through the blonde curls to hear what wisdom I might be capable of spewing forth.

I handed the man his microphone and asked instead for a sheet of yellow paper. He raised his eyebrows at me but tore the sheet off at once, handing me the yellow sheet and a pencil that had been tucked behind his ear. With the pencil I scribbled my name in a light scrawling print and wrote, "Home," on the bottom of the page.

The reporter held the page up to the crowd to a burst of applause. I walked toward the house as he held the paper up in the air and the people clapped. When I reached the porch, Mother caught up with me and hooked her arm through mine.

"Well," she said, "I guess bowling is out of the question."

We stood there for awhile listening to the cheers as I leaned against her, her blonde hair curling up around her ears. The Kingpin grinned at me from the driveway, his giant teeth shining. I waved to the crowd one last time before turning around and opening the door.

For three days the phone rang constantly. Bessie kept a vigil at the telephone, writing down the numbers of publishers and agents, all of whom, she said, were eager to have a piece of me. They wanted a tally of which poems I'd written about the walruses, what I'd be willing to reveal about my father and whether I'd consider writing my memoirs.

"Tell them I want to write," I said. "That's the only thing I know."

Newspapers printed several of my poems under photos of the dead walruses nestled behind the pylons. How odd it was to see my words there on the page where they could be read, invaded, picked apart by the world. Part of me wanted to cut them out and hide them away in a closet, but another part of me was exhilarated by it, that my words had succeeded despite my dead father and a herd of stampeding walruses. A group of poems appeared on a cable television station next to a photo of my father outside in

the driveway with a chainsaw man tucked under his arm.
The photo cut him off at the waist, but I knew his briefs
were hanging by a thread, his huge naked belly hanging
beneath the edge of the photograph. Cutting it off could
not make me forget.

The Kingpin spent days outside on the front porch talking to reporters. I watched him out the window, waving his
arms in the air and posing with bowling balls for photographs. When a reporter asked him a question about me,
he twisted in his seat, digging his hands into his pockets.
He shrugged his shoulders and absently rubbed his thumb
across the finger holes of an electric blue bowling ball.

"We tried," he said softly, "but bowling is not for her."

I sat at the window in one of Bessie's T-shirts with pink
cartoon sharks on it and drank glasses of water as I
watched him. He was at ease with the reporters, I had to
admit, and knew just when to turn his face toward the light
for photographs. At one point he stood up and turned
around to reveal his backside to the cameras. Under his
buttocks and around the hips were thick bunches where his
boxer shorts would not lay flat against his body. I breathed
a sigh of relief.

For the most part I stayed in the kitchen near Bessie and
scribbled images, fragments of poems on the backs of
envelopes. I wrote long passages about life on the road with
Bessie, the feel of unwashed hair plastered to my head, a
tusk poking at my heels. Now that the walruses were gone,
it was not easy to bring the words to the surface. The end-
less string of words had died down in my head once the
walruses had been put down. All that was left was the waiting.

I sat on an old suitcase and tried to ignore the ringing of
the telephone, the sounds of Mother clicking her heels on

the bare hardwood floors, the heavy sigh of memories. She stayed in the living room pacing back and forth, occasionally drifting in to peer in at the Kingpin holding court on the porch, but for the most part she said nothing. I kept waiting for her to ask what had happened to me, why the walruses had chased us, why I couldn't be a bowler, when I planned to take a bath. But she just walked from room to room sniffing and scuffing her shoes on the floor.

At night Bessie and I sat on the floor going over the names of the major publishers and looking at press clips from newspapers with pictures of us, my poems underneath in italics. Mother and the Kingpin sat out on the porch in the dark rubbing their feet together and whispering. A few times I thought I heard her crying, but Bessie said the Kingpin would take care of her and that it would take some time for Mother to accept the fact that bowling was not going to be part of my future.

"She still holds out hope," Bessie said. "She thinks you chose your father over her."

I looked out the window at her on the porch, leaning against the Kingpin, his teeth tiny points of light out there in the dark.

"And she chose him," I said, but I felt guilty as soon as I said it. Bessie looked down at the list of publishers and shook her head. "Besides," I said, softer this time, "I didn't really choose him. Art chose me."

Bessie nodded and pressed her fingers to my forehead, running them through the oily sweat of my bangs. I still hadn't taken a bath, felt the thick perspiration clouding my eyes, the runny fluid between my legs. No wonder Mother and the Kingpin kept their distance. The smell of me wafted through the house. But Bessie didn't care. She pressed her lips to my cheek and squeezed my shoulder.

I felt the familiar heaviness inside as I thought of all the years I'd spent waiting for my life to begin, the hours wasted struggling with massive blocks of clay trying to make sharks. The excitement of Dirk and the never-ending pizzas, the heaving splash of a walrus in the bathtub. I was a poet now, a writer; at least that was what the newspapers said. My name was there in print as proof. Art made things real, my father always said. It was a way to legitimize experience, to validate the self even in its smallest forms. Yet my life felt no more real to me than it ever had. Here I was still teetering in my adolescent body, still yearning to unlock a sealed basement door. Maybe my father was wrong; maybe writing about a walrus did nothing but deepen the pain. A walrus, I thought, was only as real as it seemed.

MOTHER AND THE KINGPIN left when the last of the reporters had drifted away, piling up their pencils and microphones to catch the next story. By the end of the week my walruses were old news. The reporters grew tired of waiting for me to come out on the lawn and recite poetry, or ad lib a story about my father that had never before been seen in print. There were still some things I wouldn't do.

"This place is not for us," I heard the Kingpin whisper the night before they left. "Bowlers can't go home again."

Bessie helped them with their suitcases while I sat at the window looking out. It was not worth the risk to venture outside to say our good-byes at the car. A wayward reporter could appear from out of nowhere to snap me unprepared or demand that I write a vignette on the spot. I was better off to say my good-byes through the window.

I was sitting with my face pressed to the glass when the Kingpin tapped at the window. It startled me, and I jumped back, my heart squeezing in my chest.

"I have something to give you," he mouthed through the glass, "something you thought you left behind."

For a minute I hesitated but then I opened the window several inches. Chips of old paint crumbled onto the floor, a stiff breeze moving over my face. He reached down to pull something out of his duffel bag and smiled at me. In the half-light of early evening, his teeth were more pale than I remembered.

"What is it?" I asked, folding my arms over my chest. I crossed my bare legs and held my breath.

He leaned down on his haunches and motioned for me to pull the window up higher. I pressed my fingers to the wood panel and stood on tiptoe, the T-shirt riding up to expose the slickness of my belly. With both hands I yanked the shirt down and stepped away from the window.

"Here," he said, "so you won't forget."

He balanced the bowling ball on the edge of the window sill. It was gray with tiny white flecks all over it, splashes of pink and orange around the finger holes. *Frances Fisk, Writer-at-Large,* in bright yellow lettering across the width of the ball.

And beneath them, *Love from Earl Anthony and Dick Weber* scribbled in bright blue magic marker. The signatures were not the same as those on the bowling pin or on the portraits in the living room. Clearly this was the Kingpin's attempt at imitation celebrity.

He winked and turned away from me, swiping saliva from the corner of his mouth with his tongue. I waited until he stepped off the porch and opened the car door before I lifted the ball and let it drop. The floor shattered, sending chips of wood flying up at my face. I laughed, opening my mouth to catch them.

"What was that?" Mother yelled. She came running through the living room and dropped her suitcase in the hallway. I kicked the ball away with my foot, sent it rolling down the hall where it smashed against the bathroom door.

"Nothing," I said. "It was nothing at all."

I smiled and adjusted my T-shirt. She cocked her head to the side, the blonde helmet still in place, and opened her mouth to say something, but then she looked down at me in my torn panties and dirty feet and must have thought better of it. I covered my mouth with my hand to keep from laughing.

We stood there for a few minutes just looking at each other. She had on her pink bowling shoes and matching shirt with hers and Bessie's names embroidered on the back. Her eyes were ringed with heavy black mascara, tiny lines dancing around the eyes. I squinted hard to stare at those lines, the way they curved down the sides of her nose, the faint etchings of age drooping her pouty mouth. These lines were new, or perhaps I'd never noticed them before. I wished for a moment that her face were made of clay, that I could dip my fingers in water and stroke her there, move my fingers in circles to smooth them away.

She turned on her heel as if to go, her eyes avoiding mine as if she had already said her good-byes. I sighed, a long slow breath, the kind that takes a long time to expel. She turned back again without a word and wrapped her arms around me. Her arms were warm around my waist, her hands delicate and smooth. I pressed my face to her neck and breathed in a warm cloud of hair spray and the Kingpin's fishy breath, the dusty reminder of bowling balls. I held her tightly and closed my eyes.

"There's always time," she whispered. "You can always change your mind."

She pressed her lips to my forehead and held them there. I thought of all the times I'd felt my father's fingers in my bangs or Bessie's warm kiss on my forehead, but rarely had Mother ever touched me there, as if she sensed she wasn't welcome to do so or couldn't bear to touch me where my father had. She took a deep breath as if sniffing for traces of clay that might have been left behind.

She let go of me suddenly and hurried out the front door. I stood listening to her footsteps on the porch thinking of all the times she'd spent out there staring at the cars passing by. I never knew what she was looking for there in the dark with her wine and cigarettes, what she might have wanted that my father hadn't been able to give. Whatever it was, the Kingpin had it. She hadn't been able to find it in anyone else—not even Bessie, and least of all me. It was something she had to find for herself.

I heard the car horn tooting as I turned away. For a minute I thought of running outside and waving wildly, letting the wind blow through the holes in my T-shirt while they sped away in a cloud of exhaust. "Mother!" I wanted to call. "Mother, good-bye!" But instead I sat on the living room floor and waited for Bessie to come back inside, for the sound of the door closing behind her, the shuffle of her steps the only sound in the stillness of the house.

THAT NIGHT I dreamed that a walrus came to my bedroom and lay next to me on the floor. In the dream I pretended to be asleep as it gyrated its way into the room, flippers slapping the floors, the house shaking under its weight. It moved closer to me until the snout was inches from my face, breathing wet and heavy spray through its whiskers. Quietly I lay there while it brushed its tusks up against my hips. I didn't move, even as it opened its great mouth and licked me with a pale black tongue. When I opened my eyes it moved slowly to the corner and slunk down, its body cracked and dry with wanting.

"You need water," I said, but then it opened its mouth in a silent scream, enveloping me in its breath.

WHEN I WAS SURE Bessie was asleep I took off my panties and T-shirt and rolled them into a ball in the corner of the room. They smelled thick, sickly, of dried sweat and lone-liness, the pungent smells of death. Slowly I tiptoed out to the hallway, covering my breasts with my hands, shivering in the cold. The floor creaked under my feet as I made it to the bathroom and closed the door behind me. For a long time I stood looking down at the floor, remembering the shape of my father's hulking back as he lay there, the thick clay footprints that had trailed down the hall. I turned on the faucet and ran my hands under the hot water, watching it mix with bits of hair and dirt that lingered there from lack of use. My heart pounded as I thought of that day, the thrill of a walrus slinking around in my head.

When the tub was full I stepped in and sat on the edge, my feet dangling in the water. I thought of all the things I knew for sure. My father had come into my bedroom at night and danced in his briefs. He made chainsaw men with his hands and touched my bangs with his fingertips. He said that art was permanent and that I would under-stand.

I flung myself into the tub all at once, the water splash-ing up over the top and running over the tile floor. *The walruses are gone, the walruses are gone,* I heard myself say. I squirmed in the water, splashing with both arms and legs, moving my head from side to side and thrashing. The water moved between my legs and through the thick hair of my armpits. I snuffed water up my nose, the heat surging through my forehead. I thought of my poor father on the floor, his hand reaching over the edge but never quite making it inside. If only he'd known, I thought, if only he'd understood that he'd gone too far and yet not far enough.

Bessie came running in her bathrobe. She stopped short when she saw me, stood over the tub with her hands reaching out.

"Sugar," she said, "what's going on?"

I shook my head and smiled at her, reached up to hold her hand and pressed it to my wet lips. Then I took a large gulp of air and held it, pulling my head down under the water, letting it move through my hair, into my ears, down the tender spots in my neck.

I kept my eyes open and stared up at Bessie as she held a hand over her mouth and shook her head. She extended her long brown arm to pull me up, but I shook my head and stayed under as long as I could. I would come up when I was ready, I thought, not when Bessie or Mother or anyone told me to. The light moved in long waves over her head as the water shimmered in front of my eyes, her face moving and changing shape above me, swimming in and out of focus. I stayed there as long as I could, until my lungs were about to burst, until there was nothing I wanted more than to pull myself up and take a giant gulp of air.

EPILOGUE

The reporter comes to interview me the day I decide to sell my father's house and everything in it. We sit in wicker chairs and sip iced tea while he scribbles with his pencils and clicks a tape recorder in my face. Bessie sits in the corner cleaning out the fish tank with a long wire scoop. Expertly she catches each goldfish one at a time and smiles to herself as they squirm in the net. She plucks each one out, her fingertips pinching the tail as she dunks them into a bowl of clear water. We smile at each other. This is the last remnant we allow of the aquarium in our lives.

"After the publication of your first book, Of Bowling Balls and Memories," *the reporter says, "you did book signings at bowling alleys. After all that bowling has signified in your life, how do you explain that?"*

He lights a cigarette and puffs a cloud of smoke over my head.

Bessie drops a goldfish on the floor. It leaps in the air out of the net, flailing from side to side under our feet before she cups it in her brown hands and deposits it into the bowl. The reporter keeps his eyes on Bessie and scribbles furiously on his pad. I start to explain that I did it as a favor to Mother, but Bessie motions for me to stop.

"Sometimes a bowling alley is the safest place to be," Bessie says. "Lots of people out there understand that."

She smiles at me and swirls the net around in the water. I slit my eyes and look out over the lawn while the reporter smokes and smokes. He flips through newspaper clippings of dead walruses on a highway, the Kingpin holding up a copy of my second book, The Dying Walrus, *me in a pair of bright yellow panties with a look of terror on my face. It's a wonder I've lived to tell about it.*

When the reviews for the first book appeared, I brought them down to the basement to sift through them. At first there was a terrible urgency to hear what others had to say about my vision, and I thought there was no better place to read them than at my father's work table next to the kiln. Bessie and I would sit cross-legged on the cold slab floor, our knees touching as we shifted the newspapers and magazines in our hands.

"Frances Fisk creates a world in which the walrus mirrors the dominance of the id in the artist's life, its massive body demanding a satisfaction that society will not allow. Only when the walrus dies is Fisk's heroine able to function in society as we know it. Yet she desperately yearns for a world in which she and the walrus are welcome, where both she and the walrus can satisfy their hungers for sexual activity and poetry without the intrusion of the normal world (i.e. bowling) upon their most basic creative needs.

"In the Fisks' world, both the walrus and the chainsaw reflect society's desire for simple solutions. In Morton Fisk's series, *Men With Chainsaws,* we see the chainsaw as reflective of one's desire to "cut things down to size," to trim off excesses in order to live a manageable life. Similarly, in Frances Fisk's debut novel, *Of Bowling Balls and Memories,* we see the walrus as a continued metaphor

of her father's life work, a monstrous being bent on crushing grand ideas of philosophy and death into the smallness
of the written word."

*Of course my father was dead and there was no way to share
these ideas with him. Bessie was my only stand-in. How was I
to know how my work related to my father's if there would
never be an opportunity to ask him? Maybe they were right, I
told Bessie, that we were both looking for easy answers in a
world too complex to understand. Or maybe we were pleading
for change, for a place where chainsaw men and walruses could
live together in a hostile world. I read the reviews over and
over and waited for a sign from my father about how I should
think of all this and still be able to write. Finally I listened to
Bessie's advice and left the reviews down in the basement in a
pile next to the kiln. Perhaps it was best not to consider these
questions at all, as Bessie said, to forget about everything but
the walruses and what they might have to tell me next.*

*The reporter asks how life has changed for me now that I no
longer struggle to sculpt sharks, now that my art is in words. I
consider telling him that the walruses come roaring when I pick
up my pen, but the rest of my life is rather quiet. Mother writes
letters from Florida but never reads my books. It is easier for her
this way, she says. Her life seems permanent enough without
having to see it in black and white staring her in the face. The
Kingpin sends boxes of bowling pins with our names on them,
but I no longer bother to open the packages. And every so often
an anonymous pizza arrives on the front porch, the steam rising in the night air.*

*But instead I tell him that my father was a genius who died
in the bathtub, and that is the great tragedy of our time. The
strain of modern dress and convention was too much for him.
All he got for trying to make things real was to find himself*

dead. He never learned how to be an artist and still live in the world.

"And you?" the reporter says. "Have you learned how?"

I glance over at Bessie and give her a tight smile. These are the kinds of questions that send Bessie and me into a fit of giggles when we see my answers printed in newspapers and magazine articles. What they don't get—what I can't bring myself to tell them—is that I've already told them everything I want them to know. My father kept on telling until there was nothing left for himself. His art revealed everything that he was, and that is why the chainsaw men got smaller and smaller until he was the only one left who could see them.

I take a deep breath and clear my throat, raise my eyebrows at Bessie. This is my cue that the interview is over. She drops the goldfish net on the floor and reaches for my hand. The reporter gathers up his notes and tape recorder and thanks me for my time. I smile at him but say nothing, the silence hanging in the air between us as he makes his way down the porch steps.

As his car pulls away, I move to the edge of the porch and stare out at the sky, the exhaust rising in slow swirls in the cool evening air. A voice whispers in the distance, deep and throaty, urging me to listen closely. I lean forward and close my eyes, letting the voice blow softly through my head:

> *"Did you ever see a walrus smile*
> *All these many years?*
> *Why, yes, I've seen a walrus smile*
> *But it was hidden by his tears."*

COLOPHON

Designed by Allan Kornblum, using Adobe Caslon for body text. Adobe's version of Caslon, redrawn for computer composition by Carol Twombly, is the best digital representation of the sturdy Dutch influenced British type designed by William Caslon in 1722. Letter for letter, many type faces are more elegant, but few look as handsome in a full-length book of prose. The Neuland was selected for display based on its resemblance to the lettering on the delightful dust jacket by Susan Nees. Thanks to Jinger Peissig for art direction, and to Kelly Kofron for laying out the dust jacket.